Puffin Books

Unbelievable?
Maybe.
But I'm telling you it's true.

The crusher had pushed all the air out of my
lungs. It was squeezing me tighter and
tighter. I knew I had only seconds to live.

Believe it or not . . .

A kid can grow younger.
Birds can bury you.
Ghosts have exams.
There are eyes in the milk.

FROM THE ONE AND ONLY PAUL JENNINGS

ALSO BY PAUL JENNINGS

THE UN BOOKS

Unreal!
Unbelievable!
Quirky Tails
Uncanny!
Unbearable!
Unmentionable!
Undone!
Uncovered!
Unseen!
Tongue-Tied!

THE CABBAGE PATCH BOOKS
illustrated by Craig Smith

The Cabbage Patch Fib
The Cabbage Patch War
The Cabbage Patch Pong
The Cabbage Patch Curse

THE GIZMO BOOKS
illustrated by Keith McEwan

The Gizmo
The Gizmo Again
Come Back Gizmo
Sink the Gizmo

Also available
in one full-colour volume,
The Fantastic and Amazing Gizmo

THE SINGENPOO BOOKS
illustrated by Keith McEwan

The Paw Thing
Singenpoo Strikes Again
Singenpoo Shoots Through
Singenpoo's Secret Weapon

Also available
in one full-colour volume,
The Many Adventures of Singenpoo

WITH MORRIS GLEITZMAN

Wicked! (series)
Deadly! (series)

Also available in single volumes

WITH TERRY DENTON
AND TED GREENWOOD

Duck for Cover
Freeze a Crowd
Spooner or Later
Spit It Out!

PICTURE BOOKS

The Fisherman and the Theefyspray
illustrated by Jane Tanner

Grandad's Gifts
illustrated by Peter Gouldthorpe

ALSO AVAILABLE

Round the Twist

Sucked In . . .
illustrated by Terry Denton

The Reading Bug
…and how you can
help your child to catch it

THE RASCAL BOOKS
illustrated by Bob Lea

Rascal the Dragon
Rascal's Trick
Rascal in Trouble
Rascal Takes Off

PAUL JENNINGS

Unbelievable!

PUFFIN BOOKS

PUFFIN BOOKS

Published by the Penguin Group
Penguin Group (Australia)
250 Camberwell Road, Camberwell, Victoria 3124, Australia
(a division of Pearson Australia Group Pty Ltd)
Penguin Group (USA) Inc.
375 Hudson Street, New York, New York 10014, USA
Penguin Group (Canada)
10 Alcorn Avenue, Toronto, Ontario, Canada M4V 3B2
(a division of Pearson Penguin Canada Inc.)
Penguin Books Ltd
80 Strand, London WC2R 0RL, England
Penguin Ireland
25 St Stephen's Green, Dublin 2, Ireland
(a division of Penguin Books Ltd)
Penguin Books India Pvt Ltd
11, Community Centre, Panchsheel Park, New Delhi-110 017, India
Penguin Group (NZ)
Cnr Airborne and Rosedale Roads, Albany, Auckland, New Zealand
(a division of Pearson New Zealand Ltd)
Penguin Books (South Africa) (Pty) Ltd
24 Sturdee Avenue, Rosebank, Johannesburg 2196, South Africa

Penguin Books Ltd, Registered Offices: 80 Strand, London WC2R 0RL, England

First published by Penguin Books Australia, 1987
First published as *Unbelievable! More surprising stories*
This edition published 2003

28 27 26 25 24 23 22 21

Text copyright © Lockley Lodge Pty Ltd, 1986
Cover design and illustrations © Bob Lea, 2003

Text designed by George Dale, Penguin Design Studio
Typeset in Berkeley Old Style by Midland Typesetters, Maryborough, Victoria
Printed in Australia by McPherson's Printing Group, Maryborough, Victoria

National Library of Australia
Cataloguing-in-Publication data:

Jennings, Paul, 1943– .
   Unbelievable.
   ISBN 0 14 130171 6.
   I. Title.
A823.3

www.puffin.com.au
www.pauljennings.com.au

To Fiona, Kirsten and Sharon Lacy

Contents

Pink Bow-tie

Well, here I am again, sitting outside the Principal's office. And I've only been at the school for two days. Two lots of trouble in two days! Yesterday I got the strap for nothing. Nothing at all.

I see this bloke walking along the street wearing a pink bow-tie. It looks like a great pink butterfly attacking his neck. It is the silliest bow-tie I have ever seen. 'What are you staring at, lad?' says the bloke. He is in a bad mood.

'Your bow-tie,' I tell him. 'It is ridiculous. It looks like a pink vampire.' It is so funny that I start to laugh my head off.

Nobody tells me that this bloke is Old Splodge, the Principal of the school. He doesn't see the joke and he gives me the strap. Life is very unfair.

Now I am in trouble again. I am sitting here outside Old Splodge's office waiting for him to call me in.

Well, at least I've got something good to look at. Old Splodge's secretary is sitting there typing some letters.

She is called Miss Newham and she is a real knockout. Every boy in the school is in love with her. I wish she was my girlfriend, but as she is seventeen and I am only fourteen there is not much hope. Still, she doesn't have a boyfriend so there is always a chance.

She is looking at me and smiling. I can feel my face going red. 'Why have you dyed your hair blond?' she asks sweetly. 'Didn't you know it is against the school rules for boys to dye their hair?'

I try to think of a very impressive answer but before I can say anything Old Splodge sticks his head around the office door. 'Come in, boy,' he says.

I go in and sit down. 'Well, lad,' says Old Splodge. 'Why have you dyed your hair? Trying to be a surfie, eh?' He is a grumpy old coot. He is due to retire next year and he does not want to go.

I notice that he is still wearing the pink bow-tie. He always wears this bow-tie. He cannot seem to live without it. I try not to look at it as I answer him. 'I did not dye my hair, sir,' I say.

'Yesterday,' says Splodge, 'when I gave you six of

the best, I noticed that you had black hair. Am I correct?'

'Yes, sir,' I answer.

'Then tell me, lad,' he says. 'How is it that your hair is white today?' I notice that little purple veins are standing out on his bald head. This is a bad sign.

'It's a long story,' I tell him.

'Tell me the long story,' he says. 'And it had better be good.'

I look him straight in the eye and this is what I tell him.

2

I am a very nervous person. Very sensitive. I get scared easily. I am scared of the dark. I am scared of ghost stories. I am even scared of the Cookie Monster on 'Sesame Street'. Yesterday I am going home on the train after getting the strap and I am in a carriage with some very strange people. There is an old lady with a walking stick, grey hair and gold wire-rim glasses. She is bent right over and can hardly walk. There is also a mean, skinny-looking guy sitting next to me. He looks like he would slit your throat for a dollar. Next to him is a kid of about my age and he is smoking. You are not allowed to smoke when you are fourteen. This is why I am not smoking at the time.

After about five minutes a ticket collector puts his head in the door. He looks straight at the kid who is smoking. 'Put that cigarette out,' he says. 'You are too young to smoke.'

The kid does not stop smoking. He picks up this thing that looks like a transistor and twiddles a knob. Then he starts to grow older in front of our eyes. He just slowly changes until he looks about twenty-five. 'How's that?' he says to the ticket collector. 'Am I old enough now?'

The ticket collector gives an almighty scream and runs down the corridor as fast as his legs can take him. The rest of us just sit there looking at the kid (who is now a man) with our mouths hanging open.

'How did you do that?' trembles the old lady. She is very interested indeed.

'Easy,' says the kid-man as he stands up. The train is stopping at a station. 'Here,' he says, throwing the transistor thing onto her lap. 'You can have it if you want.' He goes out of the compartment, down the corridor, and gets off the train.

We all stare at the box-looking thing. It has a

sliding knob on it. Along the right-hand side it says OLDER and at the left-hand end it says YOUNGER. On the top is a label saying AGE RAGER.

The mean-looking bloke sitting next to me makes a sudden lunge forward and tries to grab the Age Rager but the old lady is too quick for him. 'No you don't,' she says and shoves him off. Quick as a flash she pushes the knob a couple of centimetres down towards the YOUNGER end.

Straight away she starts to grow younger. In about one minute she looks as if she is sixteen. She *is* sixteen. She looks kind of pretty in the old lady's glasses and old-fashioned clobber. It makes her look like a hippy. 'Whacko,' she shouts, throwing off her shawl. She throws the Age Rager over to me, runs down the corridor and jumps off the train just as it is pulling out of the station.

As the train speeds past I hear her say, 'John McEnroe, look out!'

'Give that to me,' says the mean-looking guy. Like I told you before, I am no hero. I am scared of my own shadow. I do not like violence or scary things so I hand over the Age Rager to Mean Face.

He grabs the Age Rager from me and pushes the knob nearly up to the end where it says YOUNGER.

Straight away he starts to grow younger but he doesn't stop at sixteen. In no time at all there is a baby sitting next to me in a puddle of adult clothes. He is only about one year old. He looks at me with a wicked smile. He sure is a mean-looking baby. 'Bad Dad Dad,' he says.

'I am not your Dad Dad,' I say. 'Give me that before you hurt yourself.' The baby shakes his head and puts the Age Rager behind his back. I can see that he is not going to hand it over. He thinks it is a toy.

Then, before I can move, he pushes the knob right up to the OLDER end. A terrible sight meets my eyes. He starts to get older and older. First he is about sixteen, then thirty, then sixty, then eighty, then one hundred and then he is dead. But it doesn't stop there. His body starts to rot away until all that is left is a skeleton.

I give a terrible scream and run to the door but I cannot get out because it is jammed. I kick and shout but I cannot get out. I open the window but the train is going too fast for me to escape.

And that is how my hair gets white. I have to sit in that carriage with a dead skeleton for fifteen minutes. I am terrified. I am shaking with fear. It is the most horrible thing that has ever happened to me. My hair goes white in just fifteen minutes. I am frightened into being a blond. When the train stops I get out of the window and walk all the rest of the way home.

'And that,' I say to Splodge, 'is the truth.'

3

Splodge is fiddling with his pink bow-tie. His face is turning the same colour. I can see that he is about to freak out. 'What utter rubbish,' he yells. 'Do you take me for a fool? Do you expect me to believe that yarn?'

'I can prove it,' I say. I get the Age Rager out of my bag and put it on his desk.

Splodge picks it up and looks at it carefully. 'You can go now, lad,' he says in a funny voice. 'I will send a letter home to your parents telling them that you are suspended from school for telling lies.'

I walk sadly back to class. My parents will kill me if I am suspended from school.

For the next two weeks I worry about the letter showing up in the letter box. But nothing happens. I am saved.

Well, it is not quite true that nothing happens. Two things happen: one good and one bad. The good thing is that Splodge disappears and is never seen again.

The bad thing is that Miss Newham gets a boyfriend. He is about eighteen and is good-looking.

It's funny, though. Why would she go out with a kid who wears pink bow-ties?

One-shot Toothpaste

'I'm afraid this tooth will have to be filled,' said Mr Bin. 'It's badly decayed.'

Antonio's knees started to knock as he looked at the dentist's arm. He knew that Mr Bin was hiding a needle behind his back. 'Not an injection. Not that,' spluttered Antonio. But it was too late. Before he could say another word the numbing needle was doing its work.

Antonio could feel tears springing into his eyes. He stared helplessly out of the window at the huge white tooth that was swinging in the breeze. On the side of it was written:

M. T. BIN

DENTIST

The needle seemed to be taking years to go in. Mr Bin held Antonio's mouth open with one hand and slowly pushed the plunger with the other. 'Try not to move,' he said. 'You're shaking like a leaf.'

At last it was over. The dreaded needle came out. 'Rinse,' ordered Mr Bin. Antonio took a mouthful of water from the glass and tried to spit it out but his mouth was numb and he dribbled most of it down his T-shirt.

Antonio fought back the tears as Mr Bin started up the drill. He mustn't cry. It wouldn't be right for a thirteen-year-old boy to cry at the dentist's. He stared out of the window again at the giant tooth sign and opened up his mouth.

'What are you going to do for a job when you leave school?' asked Mr Bin.

'A dustman,' answered Antonio. 'I've always wanted to be a dustman.'

Mr Bin put down the drill with an amazed look on his face. 'A dustman. Did you say a dustman? Now isn't that funny? I always wanted to be a dustman when I was a boy.'

'Well, how come you ended up a dentist then?' Antonio asked.

The dentist looked around the room and then went over and shut the door. He spoke in a very soft voice. 'If you promise not to tell anyone, I'll tell you the story, seeing that you want to be a dustman too. But you must give me your solemn promise not to tell any other person. Not a soul. Do you promise?'

Antonio nodded. He couldn't say a word because Mr Bin had started drilling away inside his mouth. He closed his eyes and listened.

'When I was a boy,' said Mr Bin, 'I loved looking in rubbish bins. I just couldn't walk past one without opening it. I mean there are really some wonderful things to be found in the garbage.

'I once found a dead pig's head in our neighbour's bin. I took it home and put it on an ants' nest. They ate all the flesh off and I was left with just the skull. Next I drilled a hole in the top of it and gave it to my mother for a sugar container. She liked it so much that she never used it. She hid it away in a special place and then forgot where it was.

'All the bins in our street had something interesting about them, but Old Monty's rubbish was the strangest. I used to look in his garbage bin every Wednesday and Friday and it was always filled with the same thing. Empty toothpaste tubes. Dozens and dozens of them. They weren't your everyday tubes either. They always had the same label: ONE-SHOT TOOTHPASTE was written on every one.

'I could never work out why one old man who lived all alone would use so many tubes of toothpaste. He couldn't have spent all day cleaning his teeth. Or I should say tooth, for he only had one fusty, old green tooth right in the middle of his mouth. In fact his tooth was so scungy that I am sure he had never cleaned it since the day it first grew.

'I couldn't stop thinking about Old Monty and his empty toothpaste tubes. I just had to find out what was going on. I knew it would be no good trying to talk to him because he hated children (actually, I think he hated everyone). If you said "good morning" to him he would just tell you to clear off. In the end I decided to sneak up to his house at night and peek in the window.'

2

'One night, after my parents had gone to bed, I crept up to the side of Monty's house. It was a ramshackle, tumble-down old joint with a rusty tin roof and cobwebs all over the windows. It was a dark night and a cold wind was blowing. I was covered in goose bumps, but they weren't from the cold. I was scared stiff.

'I stumbled around until I found a window which had a chink between the curtains. Then I stood on tip-toe and peered inside. All was black in the room and at first I couldn't see anything. After a minute or two, however, I noticed something eerie, something strange, something I had never seen before. Teeth. I saw teeth.

'About twenty sets of teeth were glowing palely in the dark. They were so white that they shone like tiny, dim light globes in the blackness. They hovered in the air at various heights above the floor like fierce kites on strings.

'They were opening and shutting and waving around as if they belonged to invisible heads. That was when I realised the teeth did have heads. And bodies. I just couldn't see them because it was dark. The teeth were so clean that they gave off their own light.

'There were large pointed teeth and tiny sharp ones. There was every type of cruncher and chomper that you could think of except one. None of them belonged to people. There were no human teeth. I could tell that at once.

'Just then someone lit a candle and an amazing sight met my eyes. I saw a room filled with animals.

There were rabbits, dogs, kangaroos, wallabies and cats. Each one was in its own cage and each one possessed the whitest set of teeth I had ever seen. But the poor things – they all looked so sad. I could tell they hated being kept in those small cages. And even more, they hated what was about to happen next.

'Monty strode across the room with an evil grin on his face and a candle in his hand. "Tooth time, boys," he croaked. I could almost feel the poor animals shiver as he said it. He put the candle on a table and went over to a large cupboard and opened it. Inside were thousands of tubes of toothpaste. He took down one of the tubes. "Number 52A," he said. "Let's see if this is the mix that will make my fortune."

'Monty went over to the cage of a small rabbit and pressed a button. A red light flashed inside the cage and the rabbit poked its head out of a hole in the wire. The rabbit screwed up its nose and bared its teeth. Monty put some of the toothpaste on a brush and scrubbed away at them. I could tell that the toothpaste tasted terrible. When Monty had finished he threw a dirty old carrot to the rabbit but the poor thing couldn't eat. It was too busy trying to get the nasty taste out of its mouth.

'This was terrible. This was monstrous. How cruel. That mean old man was cleaning the teeth of animals with some foul-tasting toothpaste. He was trying it out on them to see if it was any good. I didn't think of my own safety. I didn't think of anything except those frightened creatures. I raced around to the front door and banged on it as hard as I could. "Let me in," I screamed. "Let me in and let those animals go."'

3

'The door swung open and there stood Monty, grinning at me with his fusty green tooth. He seemed pleased to see me. "Just what I need," he said. "A cheeky brat of a kid. Come in, boy, and welcome."

'I burst into the house and ran into the room where the animals were kept. "What are you doing?" I yelled. "Why are you cleaning these animals' teeth?"

'"I am inventing One-shot Toothpaste," grinned Monty. "And I am nearly there."

'"What's One-shot Toothpaste?" I shouted.

'"It's toothpaste that you only use once in your life. One go and you never need to clean your teeth again. Everyone will buy it once it's invented. All those brats who won't clean their teeth. Their parents will all buy it and I will be rich. Every time I make a new batch I have to try it out. That's why I have the animals."

'"Let the animals go," I said. "It's cruel. Try your rotten old toothpaste out on yourself."

'"I couldn't do that," said Monty. "It tastes horrible. But now I don't need the animals any more. I have you." He looked at me with a sneaky smile and pointed to an empty cage.

'Before I had a chance to move he jumped on me and grabbed me with his skinny hands. He was thin but very strong. We rolled over and over on the floor and crashed into the cupboard. Hundreds of tubes of toothpaste fell out of the cupboard and showered all over us. As we struggled on the floor many of the tubes burst open and squirted long worms of toothpaste into the air. Soon we were both covered in every colour of toothpaste you could think of. They all got mixed up and the different types smeared into horrible, smelly puddles.

'Monty grabbed the toothbrush and dipped it into the mixture. "See how you like this, boy," he hissed as he tried to shove the brush into my mouth.

'There was no way I was going to let him put mixed-up toothpastes on my teeth. I pushed Monty backwards and he fell against the wall with a grunt. He was winded and lay there gasping for breath. "Have a bit of your own medicine," I said. I plunged the toothbrush into Monty's mouth and brushed at his fusty old green tooth.'

4

'He didn't like it. Not one bit. He rolled around on the floor screaming and yelling and holding his hands up to his neck. It must have tasted foul.

'Then something happened I will never forget. Monty's tooth started to grow. It swelled up and started to stick out of his mouth. Soon it was as big as his head. A whopping big green fusty tooth. And as it grew Monty started to shrink. It was just as if the tooth was sucking his innards out. Monty shrivelled up like a slowly collapsing balloon as the tooth grew bigger and bigger. Soon it was bigger than he was. It wasn't Monty and a tooth. It was a tooth and Monty.

'The tooth continued to feed on Monty until it was as big as a full-grown man and he was only the

17

size of a pea on the end of it. Then there was a small "pop" and he was gone altogether. The super tooth lay there alone on the floor.

'I was in a daze. I didn't know what to do. I staggered over to the cages and let the animals out one at a time. Each one bounded out of the door in a panic.

'The last to go was a big kangaroo. The poor thing was in such a fright that it knocked over the table with the candle on it. In a flash the curtains caught on fire and the room was alight. The animals had all fled into the night, so I grabbed the huge tooth and lugged it out onto the lawn. The house burned to the ground before the fire brigade could even get there.'

5

'And that,' said the dentist to Antonio, 'is the end of the story. And your filling is finished. It didn't hurt much, now, did it?'

'No,' said Antonio, 'I didn't feel a thing. 'But what happened to the giant tooth?'

Mr Bin looked up at the large tooth swinging in the breeze outside with

M. T. BIN

DENTIST

written on it and said, 'That is a secret which I can't tell even you.'

Antonio walked outside and looked at the large tooth sign. It was painted white but on one corner the paint was peeling off. Underneath he could see that it was a fusty green colour. He turned round and walked home, shaking his head as he went.

Mr Bin went back into his surgery. A small girl was sitting in the chair crying. 'No needles, please,' she whimpered.

'What are you going to do for a job when you grow up?' asked Mr Bin.

'A ballet dancer,' said the little girl.

Mr Bin put down the needle with an amazed look on his face. 'A ballet dancer. Did you say a ballet dancer? Now isn't that funny? I always wanted to be a ballet dancer when I was a boy.'

'Well, how come you ended up a dentist?' the girl asked.

Mr Bin looked around the room and then went over and shut the door. He spoke in a very soft voice. 'If you promise not to tell anyone, I'll tell you the story,' he said as he picked up the needle.

There's No Such Thing

Poor Grandad. They had taken him away and locked him up in a home. I knew he would hate it. He loved to be out in his garden digging the vegies or arguing with old Mrs Jingle next door. He wouldn't like being locked away from the world.

'I know it's sad,' said Mum. 'But it's the only thing to do. I'm afraid that Grandad has a sort of sickness that's in the head. He doesn't think right. He keeps seeing things that aren't there. It sometimes happens to people when they get very old like Grandad.'

I could feel tears springing into my eyes. 'What sort of things?' I shouted. 'I don't believe it. Grandad's all right. I want to see him.'

Mum had tears in her eyes too. She was just as upset as I was. After all, Grandad was her father. 'You can see him on Monday, Chris,' she said. 'The nurse said you can visit Grandad after school.'

On Monday I went to the nursing home where they kept Grandad. I had to wait for ages in this little room which had hard chairs and smelt of stuff you clean toilets with. The nurse in charge wore a badge which said, SISTER GRIBBLE. She had mean eyes. They looked like the slits on money boxes which take things in but never give anything back. She had her hair done up in a tight bun and her shoes were so clean you could see the reflection of her knobbly knees in them.

'Follow me, lad,' said the nurse after ages and ages. She led me down a corridor and into a small room. 'Before you go in,' she said, 'I want you to know one thing. Whenever the old man talks about things that are not really there, you must say, "There's no such thing." You are not to pretend you believe him.'

I didn't know what she was talking about, but I did know one thing – she shouldn't have called Grandad 'the old man'. He had a name just like everyone else.

We went into the room and there was Grandad, slumped in a bed between stiff white sheets. He was staring listlessly at a fly on the ceiling. He looked unhappy.

As she went out of the room Nurse Gribble looked

22

at Grandad and said, 'None of your nonsense now. Remember, there's no such thing.' She sat on a chair just outside the door.

2

Grandad brightened up when he saw me. A bit of the old twinkle came back into his eyes. 'Ah, Chris,' he said. 'I've been waiting for you. You've got to help me get out of this terrible place. My tomatoes will be dying. I've got to get out.' He looked at the door and whispered. 'She watches me like a hawk. You are my only chance.'

He pulled something out from under the sheets and pushed it into my hands. It was a small camera with a built-in flash. 'Get a photo,' he said, 'and then they will know it's true. They will have to let me out if you get a photo.'

His eyes were wild and flashing. I didn't know what he was talking about. 'Get a photo of what?' I asked.

'The dragon, Chris. The dragon in the drain. I never told you about it before because I didn't want to scare you. But now you are my only hope. Even your mother thinks I have gone potty. She won't believe me that there is a dragon. No one will.'

A voice like broken glass came from the corridor outside. It said, 'There's no such thing as a dragon.' It was Nurse Gribble. She was listening to our conversation.

I didn't know what to think. It was true then. Poor old Grandad was out of his mind. He thought there was such a thing as a dragon. I decided to go along with it. 'Where is the dragon, Grandad?' I whispered.

'In Donovan's Drain,' he said softly, looking at the door as he spoke. 'Behind my back fence. It's a great horrible brute with green teeth and red eyes. It has scales and wings and a cruel, slashing tail. Its breath is foul and stinks of the grave.'

'And you've seen it?' I croaked.

'Seen it, seen it. I've not only seen it, I've fought it. Man and beast, battling it out in the mouth of Donovan's Drain. It tried to get Doo Dah. It eats dogs. And cats. It loves them. Crunches their bones. But I stopped it, I taught it a thing or two.' Grandad jumped out of bed and grabbed a broom out of a cupboard. He started to battle an imaginary dragon, stabbing at it with the broom and then jumping backwards.

He leapt up onto the bed. He was as fit as a lion. 'Try to get Doo Dah, will you? Try to eat my dog? Take that, and that, you smelly fiend.' He lunged at the dragon that wasn't there, brandishing the broom like a spear. He looked like a small, wild pirate trying to stop the enemy from boarding his ship.

Suddenly a cold, crisp voice cut across the room. 'Get back in bed,' it ordered. It was Nurse Gribble. Her mean eyes flashed. 'Stop this nonsense at once,' she snapped at Grandad. 'There is no such thing as a dragon. It's all in your head. You are a silly old man.'

'He's not,' I shouted. 'He's not silly. He's my grandad and he shouldn't be in here. He wants to get out.'

The nurse narrowed her eyes until they were as thin as needles. 'You are upsetting him,' she said to me. 'I want you out of here in five minutes.' Then she spun around and left the room.

'I've got to escape,' said Grandad as he climbed slowly back into his bed. 'I've got to see the sun and the stars and feel the breeze on my face. I've got to touch trees and smell the salt air at the beach. And my tomato plants – they will die without me. This place is a jail. I would sooner be dead than live here.'

His bottom lip started to tremble. 'Get a photo, Chris. Get a photo of the dragon. Then they will know it's true. Then they will have to let me out. I'm not crazy – there really is a dragon.'

He grabbed my arm and stared urgently into my eyes. 'Please, Chris, please get a photo.'

'Okay, Grandad,' I told him. 'I'll get a photo of a dragon, even if I have to go to the end of the earth for it.'

His eyes grew wilder. 'Don't go into the drain. Don't go into the dragon's lair. It's too dangerous. He will munch your bones. Hide. Hide at the opening and when he comes out take his photo. Then run. Run like crazy.'

'When does it come out?'

'At midnight. Always at midnight. That's why you need the flash on the camera.'

'How long since you last saw the dragon, Grandad?' I asked.

'Two years,' he said.

'Two years,' I echoed. 'It might be dead by now.'

'If it is dead,' said Grandad, 'Then I am as good as dead too.' He looked gloomily around the sterile room.

I heard an impatient sigh from outside. 'Visiting

time is over,' said Nurse Gribble, in icy tones.

I gave Grandad a kiss on his prickly cheek. 'Don't worry,' I whispered in his ear. 'If there is a dragon I will get his photo.' The nurse was just about busting her ear-drums trying to hear what I said but it was too soft for her to make out the words.

As she showed me out, Nurse Gribble spoke to me in her sucked-lemon voice. 'Remember, boy, there's no such thing as a dragon. If you humour the old man you will not be allowed back.'

I shook my head as I walked home. Poor Grandad. He thought there was a dragon in Donovan's Drain. I didn't know what to do now. I didn't believe in dragons but a promise is a promise. I would have to go to Donovan's Drain at midnight at least once. I tried to think of some other way to get Grandad out of that terrible place but nothing came to my mind.

3

And that is how I came to find myself sitting outside the drain in the middle of the night. It was more like a tunnel than a drain. It disappeared into the black earth, from which came all manner of smells and noises. I shivered and waited but nothing happened. No dragon. After a while I walked down to the opening and peered in. I could hear the echo of pinging drips of water and strange gurglings. It was as black as the insides of a rat's gizzards.

In the end I went there five nights in a row. I didn't see Grandad in that time because the nurse would only let me visit once a week. Each night I sat and sat outside the drain but not the slightest trace of a dragon appeared. It gave me time to think and I started to wonder if perhaps Grandad's story could be true. What if he had seen a dragon? It could be asleep for the winter – hibernating. Perhaps dragons slept for years. It might not come out again for ten years. In the end I decided there was only one way to find out.

I had to go in.

The next night I crept out of the back door when Mum was asleep. I carried a torch and Grandad's camera and I wore a parka and two jumpers. It was freezing.

I walked carefully along the drain with one foot on either side of the small, smelly stream that ran down the middle. It was big enough for me to stand upright. I was scared, I will tell you that now. It was

absolutely black in front of me. Behind me the dull
night glow of the entrance grew smaller and smaller.
I didn't want to go but I forced myself to keep
walking into the blackness. Finally I looked back
and could no longer see the entrance.

I was alone in the bowels of the earth in the
middle of the night. I remembered Grandad's words.
'Don't go into the dragon's lair. It's too dangerous.
He will munch your bones.'

I also remembered Nurse Gribble's words. 'There's
no such thing as a dragon.' I almost wished she was
right.

The strong beam of the torch was my only
consolation. I shone it in every crack and nook.
Suddenly the idea of a dragon did not seem silly. In
my mind I could see the horrible beast with red eyes
and dribbling saliva, waiting there to clasp me in its
cruel claws.

I don't know how I did it but I managed to walk
on for a couple of hours. I had to try. I had to check
out Grandad's tale. I owed him that much.

Finally the tunnel opened into a huge cavern. It
was big enough to fit ten houses inside. Five tunnels
opened into the cavern. Four of them were made
out of concrete but the fifth was more like a cave

that had been dug out by a giant rabbit. The earth sides were covered in a putrid green slime and deep scratch marks.

I carefully made my way into the mouth of this cave. I wanted to turn and run. I wanted to scream. I half wished that a dragon would grab me and finish me off just to get it over and done with. Anything would be better than the terror that shook my jellied flesh.

I stumbled and fell many times, as the floor was covered in the same slime as the walls. The tunnel twisted around and upwards like a corkscrew. As I progressed a terrible smell became stronger and stronger. It was so bad that I had to tie my hand-kerchief over my mouth.

Just as I was about to give up I stood on something that scrunched under my feet. It was a bone. I shone the torch on the floor and saw that small bones were scattered everywhere. There were bones of every shape and size – many of them were small skulls. On one I noticed a circle of leather with a brass tag attached. It said 'Timmy'. I knew it was a dog's collar.

As I pushed on, the bones became deeper and deeper until at last they were like a current sweeping around my knees. My whole body was shaking with fear but still I pressed on. I had to get that photo. The only way to get Grandad out of that nursing home was to prove he wasn't mad.

Finally the tunnel opened up into another cavern that was so large my torch beam could not reach the roof. And in the middle, spread out across a mountain of treasure, was the dragon.

4

His cruel white jaws gaped at me and his empty eyes were pools of blackness. He made no movement and neither did I. I stood there with my knees banging together like jackhammers.

The horrible creature did not jump up and crunch my bones. He couldn't. He was dead.

He was just a pile of bones with his wings stretched out in one last effort to protect his treasure. He had been huge and ugly. The dried-out bones of his wings were petrified in earthbound flight. His skull dripped with slime and leered at me as if he still sought to snap my tiny body in two.

And the treasure that he sought to hoard? It was poor indeed. Piles of junk. Broken television sets, discarded transistor radios, dustbin lids, old car wheels, bottles, a broken pram, cracked mirrors and twisted picture frames. There was not a diamond or a gold sword to be seen. The dragon had been king of a junk heap. He had saved every piece of rubbish that had floated down the drain.

Now I could get what I came for. I could take a photo. I stood on a smooth rock and snapped away with my camera. This was the evidence that would save Grandad. I took about ten photos before my foot slipped and the torch and camera spun into the air. I heard them clatter onto the dragon's pile of junk. The torch blinked as it landed and then flicked out. I was in pitch blackness. Alone with a dead dragon.

I felt my way carefully forward trying to find the camera. The rock on which I had stood was not a rock at all. It was a smooth type of box with rounded corners. I felt it carefully with my fingers, then I started to grope my way forward. I had to find the camera and the torch but in my heart I knew that it was impossible. They were somewhere among the dragon's junk. Somewhere under his rotting bones. I knew I would never find either of them in the dark.

As I started to grope around in the rubbish I bumped into an old oil drum. It clattered down the heap making a terrible clacking as it went.

Suddenly I felt the damp ground tremble. The noise had loosened the roof of the cave. Pieces of rock and stone started to fall from above. The cave was collapsing. The earth shook as huge boulders fell from the roof above. I had to get out before I was buried alive. I stumbled back through the rubbish to the tunnel and fought my way through the piles of bones. I often hit my head on a rock or slipped on the slimy floor. I could hear an enormous crashing and squelching coming from behind. Suddenly a roaring filled the air and a blast of air sent me skidding down the corkscrew passage. The whole roof of the cavern must have fallen in.

I skidded down the slippery tube on my backside. The floor was rough and the seat was ripped out of my pants as I tumbled down and down.

At last I landed upside down at the bottom. I was aching all over and although I couldn't see anything I knew I must be bleeding.

A bouncing noise was coming from above. Something was tumbling down after me. Before I could move, a hard, rubbery object crashed into me and knocked me down. It was the smooth box-thing that I had stood on.

I just sat there in the gurgling water and cried. It had all been in vain. I had seen the remains of the dragon and taken the photo. But the camera and the dragon and his rubbishy treasure were all buried under tonnes of rock. The dragon was gone for ever and so was Grandad's hope of getting out of the nursing home. There was no proof that the dragon had ever lived.

5

I could feel the box-thing move off down the drain. It was floating. I decided to follow it downstream and I think that it probably saved my life. By following the floating cube I was able to find my way back without a torch.

At last – wet, cold and miserable – I emerged into the early morning daylight. The whole adventure had been for nothing. Everyone would still think that Grandad was crazy and I was the only one who knew he wasn't. All I had to show for my efforts was the rubbery cube. I had no proof that a dragon had once lived in the drain.

I looked at the cube carefully. It looked like a huge dice out of a game of Trivial Pursuit except it

had no spots on it. It was heavy and coloured red.
I could see it had no lid. It was solid, not hollow.
I decided to show it to Grandad.

I carried the cube back home and had a shower.
Mum had gone to work. I got into some clean clothes
and went round to the nursing home. The mean-
eyed nurse sat in her glass prison warder's box at
the end of the corridor.

'Well,' she said sarcastically, 'where is your dragon
photo?'

'I haven't got one,' I said sadly, 'but I have got
this.' I held up the cube.

'What is it?' she snapped.

'It's from the dragon's cave,' I said weakly.

'You nasty little boy,' she replied. 'Don't think your
lies are going to get the old man out. You make sure
that when you leave that smelly box leaves too.'

I went down to Grandad's room. His face lit up
when he saw me but it soon grew sad as he listened
to my story.

'I'm finished, Chris,' he said. 'Now I will never be
able to prove my story. I'm stuck here for life.'

We both sat and stared miserably at the cube.
Suddenly Grandad sat up in bed. 'Wait a minute,' he
said. 'I've read about something like that in a book.'

He pointed at the cube. 'I think I know what it is.' He was smiling.

As he spoke, I noticed a crack appearing up one side. With a sudden snap the whole thing broke in half and a little dragon jumped out.

'It's a dragon's egg,' shouted Grandad. 'Dragon's eggs are cube-shaped.'

The little monster ran straight at my leg, snapping its teeth. It was hungry. I jumped up on the bed with Grandad and we both laughed. Its teeth were sharp.

The dragon was purple with green teeth. Smoke was coming out of its ears.

'I'm getting out of here,' said Grandad. 'They can't keep me now. We can prove I saw a dragon in the drain. This little fellow didn't come from nowhere. I'm free at last.'

'Hooray,' I shouted at the top of my voice. 'It really is a dragon.'

Just then I heard the clip, clop sound of Nurse Gribble's shoes. The little dragon stood still and sniffed. He was looking at the door. He could smell food.

Nurse Gribble stepped into the room and started to speak. 'There's no such thing . . .' Her voice turned into a shriek as the tiny new-born dragon galloped across the room and clamped its teeth onto her leg. 'Help,' she screamed. 'Help, help. Get it off. Get it off. A horrible little dragon. It's biting me.' She hopped from one side of the room to the other with the dragon clinging on to her leg tightly with its teeth. She yelled and screamed and jumped but the dragon would not let go.

Grandad headed for the door carrying his suitcase.

Nurse Gribble started to shriek. 'Don't go, don't go. Don't leave me alone with this dragon.'

Grandad looked at her. 'Don't be silly,' he said. 'There's no such thing as a dragon.'

Inside Out

'What did you get?' asked my sister Mary, looking at the video cassette in my hand.

'*Chainsaw Murder*,' I answered.

'You ratbag,' she screamed. 'You promised you would get something nice. You know I can't stand those horrible shows. I'm not watching some terrible movie about people getting cut up with chainsaws. And it was my turn. It was my turn to choose. You said you would get a love story if I let you choose.'

'It is a love story,' I told her. 'It's about a bloke who cuts up the girl he loves with a ch . . .'

'Don't give me that,' she butted in. 'It's another of those bloodthirsty, spooky, scary horror shows. You know I can't watch them. You know I can't sleep for weeks after I see one of them.' Her voice was getting louder and louder and fake tears started rolling down her face. She was hoping that Mum would hear her and come and tell me off.

'It's no use yelling,' I said. 'Mum and Dad are out. They won't be back until two o'clock in the morning. They've gone out to the movies.'

'I'll get you for this,' she said in a real mean voice. 'You just wait.' She went out of the room and slammed the door behind her. What a sister. Mary was the biggest sook I had ever met. If the slightest scary thing came on the screen she would close her eyes and cover up her ears. She just couldn't take it. Not like me. I wasn't scared of anything. The creepier the show, the better I liked it. I wouldn't even have been scared if I met a real ghost. Things like that just made me laugh.

I put the cassette into the video player and sat down to enjoy the show. It was even better than I expected. It started off looking through a window at a bloke starting up a chainsaw. Suddenly the window was spattered in blood and you couldn't see through it. The whole movie was filled with dead bodies, skeletons coming up out of graves, ghosts with no heads and people getting cut up with chainsaws. It was great. I had never had such a good laugh in all my life.

After about an hour I started to feel hungry. I went over to the pantry and made myself a peanut butter, Vegemite, banana and pickle sandwich. I wanted to put on a bit of mustard but I couldn't find any. While I was searching around for it I heard Mary come into the room. 'Changed your mind?' I asked without looking up. 'What's the matter? Are you scared up there all on your own in the bedroom?'

Then I heard a terrible sound. Mary had pushed the EJECT button on the video player. As quick as a flash she whipped out the cassette and ran out of the room with it. The little monster had nicked it. The terrible deed was done in a second. She was quicker than the villain in *Graveyard Robber* (a really good video about a freak who stole corpses). I ran up the stairs after her but I was too late. Mary slammed her bedroom door and locked it.

I banged on the door with my fists. 'Give that tape back, you creep. It's just up to the good bit where the maggots come out of the grave.'

'No way,' she said through the locked door. 'I'm not giving it back. I can hear all the screaming and groaning and creepy music from up here and I'm scared. I'll give you the video back if you go and change it for *Love Story*.'

'*Love Story!*' I shouted. 'Never. I'm not watching that mush.'

'I'm scared, Gordon,' she said. 'Please take it back.' How pathetic. She sounded just like the helpless woman in *I Married A Cannibal Chief*, a ripper movie with lots of gory bits about a bloke with a big appetite.

Mary was scared because Mum and Dad were out. That give me an idea.

'Give that tape back,' I said. 'Or I'm going out and leaving you here on your own.' There was no reply. She was being really stubborn so I turned round and walked down the stairs. I was mad at her because I really wanted to see the rest of that movie.

Just as I reached the front door she appeared at the top of the stairs. 'Come back, Gordon. Please come back. I'll be frightened here all on my own.' I kept going. She had left it too late and it was time for her to be taught a lesson.

2

As I walked down the dark street I laughed to myself. Mary was really wet. She was scared of her own shadow. She would really be freaking out alone in the house. I had a good laugh and then I started to wonder why she got so scared. I mean, I wasn't scared of anything. I had even watched *The Eyes Of The Creeping Dead* without one shiver. And yet Mary, my own flesh and blood, was exactly the opposite.

I started to think about all the horror movies I had ever seen. There wasn't one that had spooked me. Why, even if one of them had come true I wouldn't have worried. I was so used to seeing creepy things that a real ghost wouldn't have scared me. I would just tell it to buzz off without a second thought.

I walked past the 'All Night Video Shop' and down a dark lane. The moon was in and it was hard to see where I was going. Mary would have been terrified but not me. I almost hoped that something creepy would happen. I walked on and on through the night into a new neighbourhood. The houses started to thin out until at last I was on a country track which wound its way amongst the trees.

After a short while I came to something I had not expected to find out there in the bush. A letter box. It was old and battered and stood at the edge of the narrow track leading off into the dark trees. I decided to follow the track and see where it went.

The track led to an old tumble-down house. I could

see it quite clearly because the moon had come out. Its tin roof was rusty and falling in. Blackberry bushes grew on the verandah and all of the windows were broken. The front door was hanging off its hinges so there was nothing to stop me entering. I made my way into the front room. There in one corner was an old wooden bed. It had no mattress but it was a bed all the same. I was feeling tired so I staggered over to it and lay down. I wasn't scared. Not a bit. I decided that I would stay in this old shack and not go home until just before Mum and Dad got back. That would teach Mary a lesson.

I closed my eyes and lay there pretending I was the hero out of *Dark House Of Death*. I was a ghost hunter. I was invincible. Nothing could hurt me. At least that was how I was feeling at the time. That's why I hardly batted an eyelid when the candle came floating over.

3

Yes, a candle. A lighted candle. It just floated across the room and hovered next to the bed. I did nothing. I simply gazed at it with detachment. It came closer until it was only a few centimetres from my face.

I took a deep breath and blew it out. I thought I heard a gasp. Then the whole thing disappeared.

I turned over on my side and pretended to be asleep (a trick I had seen in a movie called *Blood In The Attic*). After a short while I heard a soft clinking sound coming from the next room. I ignored it. It grew into a rattling and then a clanking but still I took no notice. Then it became so loud it shook the floor and hurt my ears. 'Quiet,' I yelled. 'Can't a boy get a bit of sleep in here.' The terrible din stopped at once.

I knew something else was going to happen and I wasn't wrong. A moment later a green mist floated through the window and formed itself into a dim, ghostly haze that wafted to and fro across the room. 'You shouldn't smoke in here,' I said. 'You might set the place on fire.' The mist twirled itself around into a spiral and left the room through a knothole. This was great. This was good. It was just like what happened in *Spectre Of The Lost Lagoon*.

What happened next was a bit more creepy. I'm not denying that, but I decided I was handling the situation the right way. Whatever or whoever it was wanted me to go screaming off into the night. I decided to keep playing it cool. A huge pair of lips appeared and started to open and shut, showing nasty yellow teeth. Next, a pair of bloodshot eyes appeared, floating just above the lips. From out of the mouth came an enormous, forked tongue, dripping with saliva. The tongue licked its lips and then wormed its way over to me.

'Halitosis,' I managed to say. It obviously didn't know what halitosis was because it remained there, hovering in front of my face like a snake about to strike. 'Bad breath,' I translated. 'You've got bad breath. Just like the giant pig in *Razorback*.' I thought I heard another small sob just before the whole lot vanished. I wondered if I had hurt its feelings.

The next apparition consisted of a human skull with staring, empty eye sockets. 'Old hat,' I said. 'You'll have to do better than that.' Blood started to drip out of one eye. 'Still not good enough,' I told it. 'I saw that one in a movie called *Rotting Skull*.'

The other bones appeared and the whole skeleton began to dance up and down the room, twisting and turning as if to a wild beat. 'Not very cool,' I remarked a little unkindly. 'That went out years ago. Can't you do rap dancing?'

That last remark was too cutting. The spook just couldn't take it.

The skeleton sat down on a rickety chair and changed into a small ghost. It was the figure of a punk rocker. He was completely transparent and dressed in a leather jacket which was covered in studs. He also wore tight jeans and had a safety pin through his nose. He had a closely shaved head with a pink, mohawk hairdo.

4

He looked at me and then hung his head in his hands and shed a few tears. 'It ain't no use,' he wailed. 'I can't even put the frighteners onto a school boy. I'm doomed. I'm a failure.'

'If you will kindly go away and be quiet, I'll leave at one o'clock,' I told him. 'All I want is a bit of peace.'

He shook his head. 'You can't go. I need you for me exam. If I pass you can clear out – if yer still alive that is. But if I fail me exam, you'll have to go into suspended animation until the next one.'

'When is that?' I asked.

'Same time next year.'

'No thanks,' I replied. 'I have to get back to look after my little sister. She's at home alone and she

gets scared. As a matter of fact I think I'll leave now.'
I tried to stand up but I couldn't. It was just as if
unseen hands were holding me down.

'See,' he said. 'I aren't lettin' you go anywhere. You
stay here wiv me. If I pass me exam you can go. If
not – cold storage for you until next year.' The safety
pin in his nose waggled around furiously as he spoke.

I could move my mouth but nothing else. 'I have
to go,' I told him. 'I can't stay here for a year. I've
made a booking for a video called *Jack The Ripper*
for tomorrow night.'

'Yer better help me pass then,' he said.

'What do you have to do?'

'The Senior Spook is comin'. I have to scare a
victim, namely you. If it's scary enough, he passes
me. If it's not, he fails me. But it don't look good.
You don't scare easy. You just sit there givin'
mouthfuls o' cheek no matter what I do. I must say
it looks bad fer bof ov us. If I don't give you a good
fright I won't pass me exam and if I don't pass me
exam we'll bof have to stay here until the same time
next year.'

'I'll fake it,' I yelled. 'I'll pretend I'm scared. Then
you'll pass your exam and I can go.'

He shook his head sadly. 'No good. The Senior

Spook is very experienced. That's how he got to the top. He can pick up vibes. He'll know if you're not really scared.'

'Let me loose,' I said. 'I'll help you think of something. You could try something out of *Terror At Midnight*.'

'Yer won't nick orf, will ya?' he said, looking at me suspiciously.

'I promise.'

The unseen hands released me and I started to pace around the room. I thought of Mary. She would be frightened for sure but there was no way that this little punk ghost would be able to scare me.

'Have you seen the movie *Night Freak*?' I said. 'That had some good ideas in it.'

'No, I missed that one,' he said. 'Now quick, sit on the bed. Here comes the Boss. Our exam is about to begin.'

5

I sat down where I was told and the Senior Spook floated through the wall. He was dressed in a pin-striped suit, white shirt and black tie. He carried a black leather briefcase in his left hand and wore a pair of gold-rimmed glasses. I could see right through him. He took no notice of me at all and not much more of the punk spook. He sat down on a chair, opened his case and took out a biro and a notebook. Then he looked at his watch and said to the punk, 'You have ten minutes. Proceed.'

I could tell that the punk was nervous. He really wanted to pass this exam and to do that he had to give me a good fright. But I wasn't scared. Not a bit. All those years of watching horror videos made this seem like child's play. I was worried though because I didn't want to be put into cold storage until the same time next year when the punk could have his next exam in spooking. I tried to feel scared but I just couldn't.

The punk produced a tennis ball from nowhere and placed it on the table. Then he sprinkled some pink powder on it and said, 'Inside out, ker-proffle.' The tennis ball started to squirm on the table. A small split appeared and it turned inside out. Very impressive but not very spooky. My pulse didn't increase a jot. I could just see myself frozen for a year waiting for the punk to have his next chance. I groaned inside. My punk friend was going to have to do better than this. He had no imagination at all.

Next he produced a small sausage. He sprinkled some of the pink powder on it and again said, 'Inside out, ker-proffle.' The sausage split along its side as if it was on a hot barbecue. Then it turned inside out with all the meat hanging out and the skin on the inside. The Senior Spook wrote something in his notebook.

This wasn't good enough. It just wasn't good enough. It was more like conjuring tricks than horror. I wasn't the least bit scared. My heart sank.

The punk then produced a watermelon from nowhere. Once again he sprinkled on the pink powder. 'Inside, out, ker-proffle,' he said. The water-melon turned inside out with all of the fruit and the pips hanging off it. Once again the big shot wrote something in his notebook.

The punk looked at me. Then, without warning he threw some pink powder all over me and said, 'Inside, out, ker–.'

'Stop,' screamed the Senior Spook. Then he fainted dead away. He must have hit the floor a fraction before I did. Being a ghost he didn't hurt himself when he went down. I must have hit my head on the table just after I fainted. I didn't wake up for about half an hour.

When I woke up I looked around but the house was deserted. I couldn't find a sign of either of them except for something written in the dust on a mirror. It said, 'I got an A plus.'

I don't know how I managed to find my way back. I was so scared that my knees knocked. I jumped at every sound.

When I reached home I went to bed because Mary was watching a really creepy movie.

It was called *The Great Muppet Caper*.

The Busker

'Can you lend me ten dollars, Dad?' I asked.

'No,' he answered without even looking up.

'Aw, go on. Just till pocket money day. I'll pay you back.'

He still didn't look at me but started spreading butter onto a bread roll. He was acting just as if I wasn't there. He ate the whole roll without saying one word. It was very annoying but I had to play it cool. If I made him mad I would never get the money.

'I'll do some jobs,' I pleaded. 'I'll cut the whole lawn. That's worth ten dollars.'

This time he looked up. 'You must be crazy,' he said, 'if you think I'll ever let you near that lawn mower again. The last time you cut the lawn you went straight over about fifteen plants I had just put in. They cost me twenty-five dollars to buy and five hours to plant. You cut every one of them off at the base and now you want me to give you ten dollars.'

I knew straight away I had made a mistake by mentioning the lawn. I had to change the subject. 'It's important,' I told him. 'I need it to take Tania to the movies on Saturday.'

'That's important? Taking Tania to the pictures is important?'

'It is to me,' I said. 'She is the biggest spunk in the whole school. And she's agreed to go with me on Saturday night if . . .' Another mistake. I hadn't meant to tell him that bit.

'If what?' he growled.

'If I take her in a taxi. If I can't afford a taxi she's going to go with Brad Bellamy. He's got pots of money. He gets fifteen dollars a week from his dad.'

'Good grief, lad. You're only fifteen years old and you want to take a girl out in a taxi. What's the world coming to? When I was your age . . .'

'Never mind,' I said. 'Forget it.' I walked out of the room before he could get started on telling me how he had to walk five miles to school when he was a boy. In bare feet. In the middle of winter. And then walk home again and chop up a tonne of wood with a blunt axe. Every time he told the story it got worse and worse. The first time he told it he had to walk two miles to school. The way it was going it would soon be fifty miles and ten tonnes of wood chopped up with a razor blade.

I walked sadly out into the warm night air. Dad just didn't understand. This wasn't just any old date. This was a date with Tania. She was the best-looking girl I had ever seen. She had long blonde hair, pearly teeth and a great figure. And she had class. Real class. There was no way that Tania was going to walk to the movies or go on a bus. She had already told me it was a taxi or nothing. I had to give her my answer by tomorrow morning or she would go with Brad Bellamy. He could afford ten taxis because his dad was rich.

'I'm going for a walk down the beach,' I yelled over my shoulder. There was no answer. I might as well be dead for all Dad cared.

I walked along the beach in bare feet, dragging my toes through the water. I tried to think of some way of getting money. I could buy a Tattslotto ticket. You never knew what could happen. Someone had to win. Why not me? Or maybe I could find the mahogany ship. It was buried along the beach there under the sand but it hadn't been seen for over a hundred years. What if the sea had swept the sand away and left it uncovered that very night? And I found it? I could claim the reward of one thousand dollars. Boy, would I be popular then. I could hire a gold-plated taxi to take Tania out.

The beach was deserted and the moon was out. I could see quite clearly. I walked on and on, well away from the town and the houses. It was lonely and late at night but I wasn't scared. I was too busy looking out for the mahogany ship and thinking of how I would spend the reward money. Every now and then I could see something sticking out of the sand and I would run up to it as fast as I could. But each time I was disappointed. All I found were old forty-four gallon drums and bits of driftwood that had been washed up by the heavy surf. It's funny, I didn't really expect to find the mahogany ship. Things like that just don't happen, but in the back of my mind I kept thinking I might stumble over it and be lucky.

After a while I decided to climb up to the top of the sand dunes that ran along the beach. I knew I could see for miles from up there. I struggled to the top and sat down under a bent and twisted tree. Just at that moment the moon went in and everything was covered in darkness.

'What are you looking for, boy?' said a deep voice from the shadows.

I must have jumped at least a metre off the sand. I was terrified. There I was, miles away from any help, on an isolated beach in the middle of the night. And an unseen man was talking to me from the depths of the shadows. I wanted to run but my legs wouldn't move.

'What are you looking for, boy?' the voice asked again. I stared into the darkness under the tree and could just make out a shadowy figure sitting on the sand. I couldn't see his face but I could tell from the voice that he was very old.

I finally managed to say something. 'The mahogany ship,' I answered. 'I'm looking for the mahogany ship. Who are you?'

He didn't answer me but asked me another question. 'Why do you want to find the mahogany ship, boy?'

'The reward,' I stammered. 'There's a reward of one thousand dollars.'

'And what would you do with one thousand dollars if you had it?' the voice asked sadly.

I don't know why I didn't turn and run. I was still scared but I felt a little better and thought I could probably run faster than an old man if he tried anything. Also, there was something about him that made me want to stay. He sounded both sad and wise at the same time.

'A girl,' I said. 'There's this girl called Tania. I need the money to take her out. Not a thousand dollars, only ten. But a thousand dollars would be good.'

The old man didn't say anything for a long time. I still couldn't see him properly but I could hear him breathing. Finally he sighed and said, 'You think that money would make this girl like you? You think that a thousand dollars would make you popular?'

He made it sound silly. I didn't know what to say.

'Sit down, boy,' he commanded. 'Sit down and listen.'

I nearly ran off and left him. It was all very spooky and strange but I decided to do what he said. He sounded as if he expected to be obeyed, so I sat down on the sand and peered into the darkness, trying to see who he was.

'I am going to tell you a story, boy. And you are going to listen. When I am finished you can get up and go. But not until I have finished. Understand?'

I nodded at the dark shadow and sat there without moving. This is what he told me.

2

Many years ago there was a busker who worked in Melbourne. He stood by the railway station and played music to the people who went by. He dressed completely in flags. His trousers, coat and vest were made from flags and his bowler hat was covered with a flag. When he pushed a button a small door would open on his hat and flags would pop out.

He played a number of different musical instruments. With his feet he pushed pedals which banged three drums. He had a mouth organ on a wire near his face and he played a guitar with his hands. His music was terrible but people always stopped to watch and listen because of his small dog. The dog, whose name was Tiny, walked around with a hat in her mouth and took up the money people threw into it. Tiny had a coat made out of the Australian flag. Whenever the hat was empty Tiny would stand up on her hind legs and walk around like a person. Everyone would laugh and then throw money into the hat.

The Busker, for that is what everyone called him, was jealous of the dog. He could see that the people really stopped and gave money because of Tiny and not because of the music. But there was nothing he could do about it because he needed the money.

As the months went by The Busker became more and more miserable. He wanted people to like him and not the dog. He started to treat Tiny badly when nobody was looking. Sometimes he would blame her if the takings were poor. Often he would forget to feed Tiny for days at a time. The little dog grew thinner and thinner until at last she was so weak that she couldn't hold the hat up for the money. She had to drag it along the ground with her teeth.

Finally a man from the RSPCA came to see The Busker when he was working outside the station. 'That dog is a disgrace,' he said. 'You are not looking after it properly. It is so hungry its bones are sticking out. It is not to work again until it is healthy. I will give you three weeks to fatten it up. If it isn't healthy by then I will take it away and you will be fined.'

A crowd was standing around listening. 'Yes, it's a shame,' said a man who had been watching. 'Look at the poor little thing.' Other people started to call out and boo at The Busker. He went red in the face. Then he packed up his drums and guitar and put them in his car and drove off with Tiny.

It was a long way to The Busker's house for he

lived well out of town. All the way home he thought about what had happened.

'It's all the fault of the rotten dog,' he said to himself. 'If it wasn't for her none of this would have happened.' The further he went, the more angry he became. When he reached home he grabbed Tiny by the scruff of the neck and took her round to the back yard. In the middle of the yard was an empty well. There was no water in the bottom but it was very deep. It was so deep you couldn't see the bottom.

'I'll fix you, Tiny,' said The Busker. 'You're not allowed to work for three weeks. Very well then, you can have a holiday. A very nice holiday.' He went and fetched a bucket and tied a rope to it. Then he put Tiny into the bucket and lowered her into the well. The poor little dog whimpered and barked but soon she was so far down she could hardly be heard. When the bucket reached the bottom Tiny jumped out of the bucket and sniffed around the bottom of the well. It was damp from water that trickled down the wall but there was nothing to eat. The Busker pulled up the bucket and went inside.

Tiny looked up but all she could see was a small circle of light far above. She walked round and round the bottom of the well always gazing up at the patch of light at the top.

The next day The Busker went to work without Tiny. He had no dog to carry the hat around so he just put it on the ground for people to put their money in. But hardly anyone did. The Busker tried his best. He played every tune he could think of and he cracked jokes. But it was no good. In one day he took only fifty cents. Now he knew for sure that it was Tiny that the people liked and not him.

He went home and threw some meat down the well. He could hear the faint sound of Tiny barking far below. 'It's no good, Tiny,' shouted The Busker. 'I'm not letting you out for three weeks. That will teach you a lesson.'

Every day The Busker went to work and the same thing happened. He played his music but hardly anyone put money in the hat. 'No one likes me or my music without Tiny,' said The Busker to himself. He was angry. He wanted people to like him. It wasn't the money so much. He just wanted people to like him. Each night when he reached home The Busker threw meat down the well for poor Tiny. 'Hurry up and get fat, Tiny,' he said, 'because you're not coming out until you do.'

Tiny walked round and round at the bottom of the well. All day and night she looked up, hoping to be taken out. But no one ever came except The Busker and all he did was throw down meat once a day.

The three weeks went very slowly for The Busker. Each day he stood at the station playing his music to the people who walked by without listening. But the three weeks went much more slowly for the little dog who lay at the bottom of the well, always looking up at the sky for the help that didn't come.

At last the three weeks was up. The Busker decided to get Tiny out. He lowered the bucket down into the well but the little dog didn't know what to do. She walked around the bucket but didn't get into it. The Busker hadn't counted on this. 'Get in, you stupid dog,' he shouted. But it was so far down that Tiny could hardly hear him. In the end he had to go and have a rope ladder made. It cost him a lot of money because it was so long. And it took a long time to make. Tiny was down the well for another week before it was finished.

3

Then something happened that changed everything. The Busker won Tattslotto. A letter came telling him that he had won over a million dollars. He couldn't believe his luck. It was wonderful. The first thing he did was to take his drums, flags and guitar and throw them down the tip. He went and bought himself a new car and a stereo. Every day he went to the shops and bought himself anything he wanted. Soon the house was filled with every luxury you could think of.

All this time Tiny was still at the bottom of the well, barking and walking around and around, looking up at the world that was out of reach so far above. Each night The Busker came and threw down meat. And each night he told himself that he would get Tiny out in the morning. But when the morning came he forgot and did something else.

The truth is, The Busker was still unhappy. He had no more friends than before. When he bought things, the salesmen were nice to him. They patted him on the back and told him how wise he was to buy this or that. But as soon as he had bought their goods they lost interest and didn't want to talk to him.

In the end he realised he had only one friend in the world. Tiny. Tiny was the only one who really liked him. And he had put her down a well. He felt bad about what he had done to his little friend and he rushed to the well to get her out. The Busker climbed down the well to get Tiny. He was frightened because it was so deep but he knew that he had to go. There was a terrible smell in the well which got worse as The Busker went deeper. When he reached the bottom he put Tiny inside his jumper and started to climb back up the rope. All the way up Tiny licked The Busker's face, even though he had put the poor little dog down a well for all that time.

When he reached the top of the well The Busker put Tiny on the ground. What he saw made tears come into his eyes. Tiny's head was bent back and her eyes stared up at the sky. She couldn't straighten up her neck. It was so stiff she could only walk around looking upwards. 'I'm sorry, I'm sorry,' cried The Busker. 'What have I done? Forgive me, Tiny, forgive me.' Tiny licked The Busker on the face.

From that time on Tiny always walked with her head bent back staring at the sky. No vet and no doctor could do anything about it. She had been down the well too long and her neck was fixed in a bent back position for the rest of her life.

The Busker looked after Tiny well from that time on. He fed her the best food and took her with him everywhere he went. Tiny trotted around after The Busker, wagging her tail, even though her neck was bent back and her head stared up at the sky.

The Busker had all the love of the little dog even though he had treated her so badly. But it still wasn't enough. He wanted people to like him. 'What good am I,' he said to Tiny, 'when my only friend is a dog?' He became more and more miserable until one day he hit upon an idea. A great idea. Or so he thought. He put an advertisement in the newspaper which said:

TO GIVE AWAY

FREE MONEY

$1.00 PER PERSON

COME AND GET IT

2 ROSE ST, MELTON

EVERY DAY 9.00 AM

'Tiny,' said The Busker, 'the crowds will like me now. This time I will give them money instead of them giving it to me. I will give away half of all

I have. I don't need a million dollars. Half of that
will do. Those who need money can come and get
a dollar each whenever they like.'

The next morning The Busker set up a tent in his
front yard. Inside he put a table and a chair and a
bucket full of one-dollar coins. He hung a notice
outside which said:

FREE MONEY

$1.00 EACH

At nine o'clock two scruffy-looking boys came in.
'Where's the free money, Pop?' said one of them.
This wasn't what The Busker had expected. He didn't
really want children. Especially rude ones. But he
had to keep his word so he took a one-dollar coin
from the bucket under the table and gave it to the
boy. The boy looked at it carefully and said to his
friend, 'It's real.' Then he turned around and ran out
of the tent. The other boy held out his hand, snatched
his coin and disappeared out of the tent before The
Busker changed his mind.

Soon the tent was filled with more and more
children. The word had spread quickly and every
child in the neighbourhood was there. 'Form a line,'
yelled The Busker. 'And no pushing.' The children

were jostling and shoving and some were trying to push in.

The Busker was upset at the rudeness of the children. The first three simply grabbed the money and ran but the fourth child, a girl with big, brown eyes, said, 'Gee, thanks. Thanks a lot.' She turned round to walk out of the tent but The Busker called her back.

'Here,' he said, handing her another dollar. 'You are a very polite little girl. The only one who has said thanks.'

The next girl in the line heard what was said. After The Busker handed her a one-dollar coin she said, 'Thanks a lot, Mister,' and then stood there without moving.

'What are you waiting for?' asked The Busker.

'My other dollar,' said the girl. 'I said thanks too. So I should get two dollars as well.'

The Busker sighed and handed her another dollar. After that all of the children discovered their manners and said, 'Thanks.' The Busker had to give all of them two dollars. He smiled to himself. At least they were grateful.

The line grew longer and longer. Soon it reached all the way down the street. After about fifty children had taken their two dollars an old woman came to the front of the queue. The Busker handed her a dollar. She looked at it and said, 'Thank you, love. You are a very kind man. Very kind indeed.'

The Busker smiled and gave her another five dollars. He was pleased that she liked him so much.

As the morning passed, more and more adults joined the queue. The ones who were very polite received more money. The Busker gave fifty dollars to one young woman who said, 'What a wonderful, generous and good man you are.'

'This is more like it,' he thought to himself. 'People really like me. They can see I am really a good man.' He gave Tiny a pat on the head. He didn't even mind when the people in the line paid attention to Tiny. He wasn't jealous of Tiny now that he had his own admirers.

By lunch time the bucket of money was empty. The Busker put up another sign which said:

CLOSED.

GONE TO THE BANK

FOR MORE MONEY

The Busker took out two buckets of coins from the bank. 'You had better give me some notes as well,' he said to the teller. He took out ten thousand dollars' worth of notes. When he reached home he found the queue had grown to a couple of kilometres long. It went down the street and round the corner. As he went by people waved and a cheer went up. 'Good old Mister Busker,' someone yelled out.

4

Mister Busker. No one had ever called him that before. He felt wonderful. He went into the tent and started handing out more money. Most people received two dollars but the ones who said especially nice things got more. One old man came in, knelt at The Busker's feet and kissed his shoes. 'Oh Great One,' he said. 'I give thanks to you for your great compassion and generosity.'

The Busker was moved. 'There is no need for that,' he said. Then he gave the old man two hundred dollars. The news soon spread along the line. The more good things you said about The Busker, the more you got. A lot of people left the queue because they couldn't bring themselves to do it. But plenty more took their places. Soon everyone was getting at least twenty dollars.

At five o'clock The Busker put up a notice saying he had closed for the night and would be back in the morning. He went inside and sat down. He was very tired and soon fell asleep in the chair. At midnight he was woken up by a noise outside on the street. He went over to the window and looked out. He got a terrible shock. The people were still there in a long queue. They were sitting on the footpath in sleeping bags and blankets. Some had even put up small tents. A man in a van was selling pies, hot dogs and ice creams. No one wanted to lose their place in the queue and they were all staying for the night. It was like a crowd waiting to buy tickets to see a pop star. The Busker grinned. He felt like a celebrity. All of those people were there because of him.

In the morning a television crew came. They did interviews with The Busker and he was on the evening news. People came from everywhere to see the sight. The police arrived to control the traffic and keep the crowds in order. The queue grew longer and longer. And The Busker gave out larger and larger amounts of money. He had to. The people expected it when they said nice things to him. They went to lots of trouble. Some held up signs with his name on. Others had done drawings of him. One group had formed a band and sang a song saying what a great person The Busker was. Two students had made up a poem. He gave them two hundred dollars each.

On the third day the queue was four miles long. On the fifth day it was six miles long. People had to wait for three days to reach the front and The Busker had given away over half a million dollars. The money was brought every morning from the bank in an armoured car. Tiny ran up and down the line licking everyone with her little turned-up head.

At the end of the week the armoured car brought a large box of money. 'I will need one hundred thousand dollars to see me over the weekend,' said The Busker.

'I'm sorry,' said the bank manager, 'but there are only ninety thousand dollars left. If I were you I would stop now and keep some for myself.' The Busker knew that this was good advice. But he couldn't keep it. The crowd all expected money. Some of them had been waiting in line for three days and three nights. He tried to cut back and give each person less but he couldn't. They all knew what each compliment was worth. Two hundred dollars for a good song about the busker and fifty dollars for a drawing of him. He tried to give less but they started complaining and yelling that it wasn't fair. They said they were being cheated.

The Busker was sick of it. He realised that they didn't really like him. He was tired of hearing people tell him how good he was. But he had to keep going.

Finally the terrible moment came. He ran out of money. There wasn't one cent left. He wrote a sign which said:

OUT OF MONEY

He hung the sign on the tent door and ran into the house with Tiny. The news spread down the line like wildfire. 'There is no more money,' they yelled. The line broke up and the mob charged up to the house. They started yelling and banging on the door. The Busker was scared out of his brain. Someone threw a rock through the window and glass scattered all over the floor.

'Cheat,' he heard someone yell.

'Robber.'

'I've been waiting in the freezing cold for two nights.'

'Get him. Teach him a lesson.'

Another rock smashed through the window. The door was rattling and shaking. The Busker knew it would soon collapse. He ran out of the back door, followed by Tiny. The yard was empty and there was nowhere to hide. He could hear the mob smashing and crashing around inside the house. He had to hurry. Then he saw the well with the rope ladder still hanging down inside. He ran over to it and climbed down, leaving Tiny at the top. He was only just in time. The angry crowd burst into the back yard yelling and shouting.

When they saw that he had escaped they went crazy. They smashed up the house and stole all The Busker's new purchases. They broke everything they could get their hands on. One group even destroyed the back fence and the top of the well. Someone untied the rope ladder and let it go. They had no idea that, far below, the terrified Busker was hiding at the bottom.

After a while the police managed to control the mob and send them home. But it was too late to save the house. When darkness came it was a complete ruin. The Busker looked up and saw the moon. He thought it would be safe to call out for

help. He yelled and yelled at the top of his voice but
no one answered. Nobody could hear him, for the
well was too deep. No one knew he was there.
Except Tiny.

5

Days passed and no help came. It was cold and dark
and smelly at the bottom of the well. The Busker
would have starved to death if it hadn't been for
Tiny. The little dog ran off in search of food. It was
very difficult, for with her head bent back she had
trouble picking anything up in her mouth. She had to
lie down on her side, grasp a piece of food in
her teeth and then stand up. After this she would
trot to the well with an old bone or piece of stale
bread and drop it down the well.

The days turned into weeks and still no help came.
The Busker stayed alive by eating whatever Tiny
dropped down the well. Sometimes it was a piece of
rotten meat from a dustbin or a gnarled old bone left
by another dog. Once Tiny dropped down a dead cat.
Whatever it was, The Busker had to eat it or starve.

In all this time, Tiny gave everything she found
to the Busker. She ate practically nothing herself.

After a month she was skin and bone and so weak she could hardly drag herself to the well.

The Busker shouted and shouted every day but no one came. He yelled up at the sun, at the clouds, at the moon so far above. But no one answered. Then, one day, a terrible thing happened. Nothing was dropped down the well. No bone, no scraps, nothing. The next day was the same. And the day after that. The Busker licked the water off the wet wall but he had nothing to eat. He knew that his time had come. He couldn't last much longer. He grew weaker and weaker. And he wondered what had happened to Tiny.

At the end of the fifth week The Busker decided to give one more loud shout. His voice was almost gone. 'Help,' he screamed. 'Help.'

He peered up at the small dot of light above. Was that a head looking down? Was that a voice? He strained to listen.

'Hang on,' said a faint voice. 'We will soon have you out.' He was saved.

A little later a steel cable came down the well. There was a small seat on the end. The Busker sat on it and yelled up the well. 'Take me up. Take me up.'

When he reached the top he blinked. The bright light hurt his eyes but he managed to see four or five men with a tow truck and a winch. They were staring at this wild, smelly, dirty man that had come out of the well. 'We had better get you to hospital,' said one of the men. 'You don't look too good.'

'You're lucky to be alive,' said another. 'I never would have heard you if it wasn't for that poor little dog lying over there. I came over to see if it was still alive and heard you calling out.'

The Busker ran over to where the little dog lay on the ground. She was dead. She had starved to death because she had dropped every piece of food she could find down to The Busker. Tears fell down his tangled beard. He picked Tiny up in his arms. 'You can leave me,' he said to the men. 'I will be all right.'

He buried Tiny in a small grave, there in the back yard. On a piece of wood he wrote:

MY FRIEND TINY

R.I.P.

Then The Busker shuffled off. He was never seen again.

6

'And that is the end of the story,' said the old man.

I had forgotten where I was. Sitting there on a
sand dune at the beach in the middle of the night.
The story had completely taken me in. I looked at
the old man but I still couldn't see this face. I wanted
to ask him questions. I wanted to know if the story
was true. I wanted to know what happened to The
Busker. But I never got the chance.

'Go now, boy,' said the old man. 'That is the end
of the story. Go and leave me alone. I am tired.'

I didn't want to go but he sounded as if he meant
it. I stood up and walked away along the top of the
sand dune. After I had gone a little way the moon
came out. I turned around and looked back at the
tree where the old man had told the story. I could
see him clearly. He had a white beard and was
standing there in the moonlight looking up into the
tree. Then he walked away, now looking up at the
stars and the moon. With a shock I realised his neck
was fixed back. He couldn't move it. He was destined
to spend all his days looking up, as he had looked
up that well so many years ago.

The story was true. And the old man was The

Busker. I watched him shuffle away with his bent neck. Then the moon went in and he was gone.

I ran home as fast as I could and jumped into bed. But I couldn't sleep. I lay there thinking about the sad, strange tale of Tiny and The Busker who had tried to use money to make people like him.

The next morning I met Dad on the stairs. He pushed ten dollars into my hand. 'Here you are, Tony,' he said. 'If Tania won't go out with you unless you take her in a taxi, you might as well have the money.'

'Thanks, Dad,' I said.

I stuffed the ten dollars into my pocket. Then I went round to Tania's house and told her to go jump in the lake.

Souperman

'Look at this school report,' said Dad. 'It's a disgrace. Four D's and two E's. It's the worst report I have ever seen.'

He was starting to go red in the face. I knew I was in big trouble. I had to do something. And fast.

'I did my best,' I said feebly.

'Nonsense,' he yelled. 'Look what it says down the bottom here. Listen to this.'

Robert could do much better. He has not done enough work this term. He spends all his time at school reading Superman comics under the desk.

'That's it,' he raved on. 'That's the end of all this Superman silliness. You can get all those Superman comics, all those posters and all the rest of your Superman junk and take it down to the Council rubbish bin.'

'But Dad,' I gasped.

'No buts, I said *now* and I mean *now*.' His voice was getting louder and louder. I decided to do what he wanted before he freaked out altogether. I walked slowly into the bedroom and picked up every one of my sixty Superman comics. Then I trudged out of the front door and into the corridor. We lived on the first floor of the high-rise flats so I took the lift down to the Council rubbish bin. It was one of those big steel bins that can only be lifted up by a special garbage truck. I could only just reach the top of it by standing on tip-toes. I shoved the comics over the edge and then caught the lift back to the first floor.

That was when I first met Superman.

He was making a tremendous racket in flat 132b. It sounded as if someone was rattling the window. It can be very dangerous banging on the windows when you live upstairs. At first I thought it was probably some little kid trying to get outside while his mother was away shopping. I decided to do the right thing and go and save him. I pushed open the door, which wasn't locked, and found myself in the strangest room I had ever seen.

The walls of the flat were completely lined with cans of soup. Thousands and thousands of cans were stacked on bookshelves going right up to the ceiling. It was a bit like a supermarket.

Then I noticed something even stranger. I looked over at the window and saw someone trying to get in. I couldn't believe my eyes. It was him. It was really him. My hero – Superman. In person.

He was clinging to the outside ledge and trying to open the window. He was puffing and blowing and couldn't seem to lift it up. Every now and then he looked down as if he was frightened of falling. I ran over to the window and undid the catch. I pulled up the window and Superman jumped in.

2

He looked just as he did in the comics. He was wearing a red cape and a blue-and-red outfit with a large 'S' on his chest. He had black, curly hair and a handsome face. His body rippled with muscles.

'Thanks,' he said. 'You came just in time. I couldn't hang on much longer.'

My mouth fell open. 'But what about your power?' I asked him. 'Why didn't you just smash the window open?'

He smiled at me. Then he held one finger over

his mouth and went over and closed the door I had left open. 'My power only lasts for half an hour,' he said. 'I had to go all the way to Tasmania to rescue a woman lost in the snow. I only just made it back to the window when my power ran out. That's why I couldn't get the window open.'

'Half an hour?' I said. 'Superman's power doesn't last for half an hour. It lasts for ever.'

'You've been reading too many comics,' he responded. 'It's S-o-u-p-e-r-m-a-n, not S-u-p-e-r-m-a-n. I get half an hour of power from each can of soup.'

I started to get nervous. This bloke was a nut. He was dressed up in a Superman outfit and he had the story all wrong. He thought Superman's power came from drinking cans of soup. I started to walk towards the door. I had to get out of there.

'Come back, and I'll show you,' he said. He went over to the fridge and tried to lift it up. He couldn't. He strained until drops of sweat appeared on his forehead but the fridge didn't budge. Next he picked up one of the cans of soup and tried to squeeze it. Nothing happened. He couldn't get it open.

'See,' he went on. 'I'm as weak as a kitten. That proves that I have no power.'

'But it doesn't prove that you're Superman,' I said.

He walked over to a drawer and took out a bright blue can opener. Then he took out a book and flipped over the pages. 'Here it is,' he exclaimed. 'Lifting up refrigerators. Pea and ham soup.'

He took down a can of pea and ham soup from the shelf and opened it up with the bright blue can opener. Then he drank the lot. Raw. Straight out of the can.

'Urgh,' I yelled. 'Don't drink it raw.'

'I have to,' he said. 'I don't have time to heat it up. Just imagine if I got a call to save someone who had fallen from a building. They would be smashed to bits on the ground before the soup was warm.'

He walked over to the fridge and lifted it up with one hand. He actually did it. He lifted the fridge high above his head with one hand. I couldn't believe it. The soup seemed to give him superhuman strength.

'Fantastic,' I shouted. 'No one except Superman could lift a fridge. Do you really get your power from cans of soup?'

He didn't answer. Instead he did a long, loud burp. Then he held his hand up over his mouth and went red in the face. 'Sorry,' he said. 'I've got a stomach ache. It always happens after I drink the soup too quickly. I'll just nick into the bathroom and get myself an Alka Seltzer for this indigestion.'

Indigestion? Superman doesn't get indigestion. He is like the Queen or the Pope. He just doesn't have those sort of problems and he doesn't burp either. It wouldn't be right. That's when I knew he was a fake. I decided to try the soup out myself while he was in the bathroom and prove that it was all nonsense.

I looked at the book which had the list of soups. There was a different soup named for every emergency. For burst dams it was beef broth. For stopping trains it was cream of tomato. Celery soup was for rescuing people from floods.

I decided to try the chicken soup. It was for smashing down doors. I picked up the bright blue can opener and used it on a can of chicken soup I found on the top shelf. I drank the whole lot. Cold and raw. It tasted terrible but I managed to get it down. Then I went over to the door and punched it with my fist.

Nothing happened to the door but my poor fingers were skinned to the bone. The pain was awful. My eyes started to water. 'You fake,' I yelled through the bathroom door. 'You rotten fake.' I rushed out of the flat as fast as I could go. I was really mad at that phoney Souperman. He was a big disappointment. I wished I could meet the real Superman. The one in the comics.

3

My comics! I needed them badly. I wanted to read about the proper Superman who didn't eat cans of raw soup and get indigestion. I wondered if the garbage truck had taken the comics yet. There might still be time to get them back. It had taken me three years to save them all. I didn't care what Dad said, I was going to keep those comics. I rushed down to the Council bin as fast as I could.

I couldn't see inside the bin because it was too high but I knew by the smell that it hadn't been emptied. I jumped up, grabbed the edge, and pulled myself over the top. What a stink. It was putrid. The bin contained broken eggshells, old bones, hundreds of empty soup cans, a dead cat and other foul muck. I couldn't see my comics anywhere so I started to dig around looking for them. I was so busy looking for the comics that I didn't hear the garbage truck coming until it was too late.

With a sudden lurch the bin was lifted into the air and tipped upside down. I was dumped into the back of the garbage truck with all the filthy rubbish. I was buried under piles of plastic bags, bottles and kitchen scraps. I couldn't see a thing and I found it difficult to breathe. I knew that if I didn't get to the top I would suffocate.

After what seemed like hours I managed to dig my way up to the surface. I looked up with relief at the flats towering above and at the clouds racing across the sky. Then something happened that made my heart stop. The rubbish started to move. The driver had started up the crusher on the truck and it was pushing all the rubbish up to one end and squashing it. A great steel blade was moving towards me. I was about to be flattened inside a pile of garbage. What a way to die.

'Help,' I screamed. 'Help.' It was no use. The driver couldn't see me. No one could see me. Except Souperman. He was sitting on the window ledge of his room and banging a can of soup on the wall. He was trying to open it.

The great steel blade came closer and closer. My ribs were hurting. A great pile of rubbish was rising around me like a swelling tide and pushing me upwards and squeezing me at the same time. By now I could just see over the edge of the truck. There was no one in sight. I looked up again at Souperman. 'Forget the stupid soup,' I yelled. 'Get me out of here or I will be killed.'

Souperman looked down at me from the first-floor window and shook his head. He looked scared. Then, without warning, and with the unopened can of soup still in his hand, he jumped out of the window.

Did he fly through the air in the manner of a bird? No way. He fell to the ground like a human brick and thudded onto the footpath not far from the truck. He lay there in a crumpled heap.

I tried to scream but I couldn't. The crusher had pushed all the air out of my lungs. It was squeezing me tighter and tighter. I knew I had only seconds to live.

I looked over at Souperman. He was alive. He was groaning and still trying to open the can of soup. From somewhere deep in my lungs I managed to find one more breath. 'Leave the soup,' I gasped, 'and turn off the engine.'

He nodded and started crawling slowly and painfully towards the truck. His face was bleeding and he had a black eye but he kept going. With a soft moan he pulled himself up to the truck door and opened it. 'Switch off the engine,' I heard him tell the driver. Then everything turned black and I heard no more.

The next thing I remember was lying on the footpath with Souperman and the driver bending over me.

'Don't worry,' said Souperman with a grin. 'You'll be all right.'

'Thanks for saving me,' I replied. 'But you're still a phoney. The real Superman can fly.'

'I can fly,' he told me, 'but I couldn't get the can of soup open. When you rushed out of my flat you took something of mine with you. Look in your pocket.'

I felt in my pocket and pulled out a hard object. It was a bright blue can opener.

The Gumleaf War

The park ranger looked out of the train window and said, 'It's a hot summer. We'll have bushfires this year for sure.'

No one in the carriage answered him. They were all too busy looking at me and my nose. They weren't looking straight at me. They were straining their eyeballs by trying to look out of the corner of their eyes. I didn't pay any attention to them. If they wanted to be sticky-beaks, that was their business and there was nothing I could do about it. I was used to people staring at me but it still made me embarrassed. After all, I couldn't help it. I didn't ask to have the longest nose in the world. It happened by accident and it wasn't my fault.

Actually, I had only had the nose for three months. But three months is a long time when your nose has been stretched to seven centimetres long. Every day is filled with humiliation and pain because of people staring and smiling to themselves.

It all started one night when I went down to the kitchen to get myself a snack from the pantry. Dad and Mum were asleep so I crept down the stairs as quietly as I could. The pantry had two swinging doors which closed in the middle. I opened them a few centimetres and poked my nose through, looking at all the goodies within. Suddenly, someone pushed me from behind and I fell onto the doors, slamming them shut. The only problem was, my nose was stuck between them. The pain was terrible and there was blood everywhere. My screaming just about brought the house down and Dad and Mum rushed into the kitchen. Dad shoved me in the car and raced me off to hospital while Mum stayed home and told my little brother off for pushing me in the back and causing all the trouble.

The damage to my nose was monstrous. It was stretched from its normal three centimetres to seven. It stuck out on the front of my face like the bonnet of a car in front of the windscreen. I could see my own nose quite clearly without even using a mirror or going cross-eyed. And to make matters worse, the doctors said nothing could be done for another three years when I had stopped growing. They weren't willing to operate on it for three whole years. Three years of walking around with my own personal flag-pole. I felt ill at the thought of it.

I only lasted one day back at school. Most kids were pretty good about it. They tried not to stare at me and only peered at my nose when they thought I couldn't see them. But people have to look at you when you talk and I could see some of them were having a hard time not to crack up laughing. And then there were those who were downright mean. One girl made a smart remark about the only boy in the world who had to blow his nose with a bedsheet.

When I got home from school I gave it to Mum straight. 'I'm not going back to school,' I said. 'No way. I've finished with school for three years. I'm not going to be the laughing stock of Terang High.'

Mum and Dad tried everything to get me back at school. They tried bribes, but I wouldn't take them. Dad lifted me into the car and dumped me at the school gate but I just walked home again. They brought in a psychologist, a nice bloke who spent hours and hours talking to me. But nothing worked. In the end they decided to send me for a holiday with Grandfather McFuddy, who lived all alone in a shack high in the mountains. They thought a spell in the country might bring me back to my senses.

So there I was, sitting in the train on the way to Grandfather McFuddy's with a carriage load of people staring at me out of the corner of their eyes. Besides the ranger there was a clergyman with a white dog-collar around his neck, an old woman of about thirty-five and a girl about my age. The girl was biting her tongue trying to stop herself from laughing at my nose. In fact the only passenger who wasn't interested in my nose was the park ranger. He just kept mumbling to himself about how dry it was and how there were going to be bad bushfires this year.

2

Grandfather McFuddy was waiting for me at the station with a horse and trap. A horse and trap. That gave me a surprise for a start. I didn't think anyone drove around in a horse and trap any more. But that was nothing compared with what was to come. Grandfather McFuddy turned out to be the strangest old boy I had ever met. He was dressed in dirty trousers held up with a scungy pair of braces. He had a blue singlet and a battered old hat which was pulled down over his whiskery face. His false teeth were broken and covered in brown tobacco stains. He cleared his throat and spat on the ground. 'Git up here, boy,' he said. 'We have to git back before dark.'

I don't know how Grandfather McFuddy recognised me because I had never met him before. I guess he recognised my nose from Mum's letters. We rattled along the dusty road which wound its way through the still gum forest. 'Thanks for having me for a holiday, Grandfather,' I said.

Grandfather grunted and said, 'Call me McFuddy.' He wasn't a great one for talking. I told him all about my nose and what had happened at school but he made no comment. Every now and then he would cough terribly and spit on the ground. He was a fantastic spitter. He could send a gorbie at least four metres. A couple of times he stopped the horse and rolled himself a cigarette.

After a while the trees turned into paddocks and the road started to wind its way upwards. There was only one house, if you could call it a house, on the whole road. It was really a tumble-down old shack with a rusty iron roof and a rickety porch. McFuddy stopped the cart before we reached the shack. 'Cover your ears, boy,' he said to me.

'What?' I asked.

'Block your ears. Put your hands over your ears while we go past Foxy's place,' he yelled.

'Why?' I wanted to know.

'Because I say so,' said McFuddy. He put his hand in his pocket and fished out a dirty wad of cotton wool. He tore off two pieces and stuffed them in his ears. Then we went slowly past the old shack, me with my hands over my ears and McFuddy with cotton wool sticking out of his. The horse was the only one of us who could hear. An old man ran out onto the porch of the shack and started shaking his fist at us. He was mad about something but I didn't know what. I was shocked to see that the old man had cotton wool in his ears as well. There was one thing for sure, I told myself: this was going to be a very strange holiday.

McFuddy stood up in the cart and started shaking his fist back at the other old man. Then he sat down and drove on, grumbling and mumbling under his breath.

I looked round at the shack to see what the angry old man was doing. All I could see was the top of his bald head. He was bending over, peering through a telescope set up on the porch. It was pointed at another old shack higher up the mountain.

'He's looking at my place,' said McFuddy. 'That's my place up there.' My heart sank. Even though McFuddy's shack was about a kilometre away I could see it was a ramshackle, neglected heap. There were rusty cars, old fridges and rubbish all around it. The weatherboards were falling off and the last flake of paint must have peeled off about a hundred years ago.

We went inside the shack and McFuddy showed me my room. It was the washroom. It had a broken mangle and an empty trough. On the floor was a dusty striped mattress and an old grey blanket. The whole place was covered in cobwebs and the windows were filthy dirty. In the kitchen I noticed a telescope pointing out of a window. A little patch had been cleaned on the window pane to allow the telescope to be aimed down the hill at Foxy's shack.

'I'm going to put in some fenceposts in the top paddock,' said McFuddy. 'You can have a look around if you want, boy, but don't go down near Foxy's place. And don't git lost.' He went out into the hot afternoon sun, banging the door behind him.

I wandered around McFuddy's farm, which didn't take long, and then decided to go and explore a small forest further up the hill. I saw a brown snake and a couple of lizards but not much else. In the distance I could hear McFuddy banging away at his fenceposts. Then I heard something else quite strange. It was music. Someone was playing a tune but I couldn't work out what sort of instrument it was. Then it came to me. It was a gumleaf. Someone was playing 'Click Go The Shears' on a gumleaf.

I sat down on a log and listened. It was wonderful listening to such a good player. The tune wafted through the silent gum trees like a lazy bee. I strained my eyes to see who it was but I couldn't see anyone. Then, suddenly, I felt a pain in my left hand. I looked down and saw a deep scratch. It was bleeding badly. I wondered how I had done it. I thought I must have scratched it on a branch. I forgot all about the music and ran back to the shack as fast as I could.

McFuddy was sitting in the kitchen having a cup of tea. He was as angry as a snake when he saw the cut. 'How did you do it?' he yelled.

'I don't know,' I answered. 'I just noticed it when I was sitting on a log.'

'Was there music?' he shouted. 'Did you hear music?'

'Yes, someone was playing a gumleaf. A good player too.'

McFuddy went red in the face. 'They were playing "Click Go The Shears" weren't they?' he said. I nodded. He jumped out of his chair and ran over to the wall and took down a shotgun. 'That rat Foxy,' he spluttered. 'I'll get him for this. I'll fix him good.' He ran over to the door and fired both barrels of the shotgun somewhere in the direction of Foxy's shack. It went off with a terrific bang that rattled the windows.

I ran outside and looked down the mountainside. Far below I could see Foxy's shack. A tiny figure was standing on the porch and pointing something up at us. There was a small flash and then the dull sound of another shotgun blast echoed through the hills.

'Missed,' said McFuddy. 'Missed by a mile.' He went back in the kitchen chuckling to himself. I wasn't surprised that Foxy had missed. I wasn't surprised that either of them had missed. Shotguns aren't meant to be used over long distances. There was no way they could have hit each other.

'What's going on?' I asked. 'Foxy didn't give me the scratch. There was no one near me at all. I didn't see one person the whole time I was away. It wasn't his fault. It was an accident.'

McFuddy didn't answer for a while. He was eating a great slab of bread covered in blackberry jam. He pushed his false teeth between his lips and fished around under them with his tongue, cleaning out the blackberry seeds. When he had finished he said, 'Don't git yerself into something yer don't understand. Foxy is lower than a snake's armpit. He caused that cut and that's that.'

'But,' I began.

'No buts. And don't go wandering off again without my permission.'

That was the end of the discussion. He just wouldn't say any more about it. That night I went to bed on the old mattress. I tossed and turned for a while but at last I went off to sleep.

3

In the morning McFuddy had a terrible cold. He was coughing and sneezing and spitting all the time. His nose was as red as a tomato. He was in a bad temper.

'Foxy's been here,' he yelled. 'He's given me the flu. He came when I was in bed and I couldn't git out quick enough.

'Didn't yer hear it boy? Didn't yer hear the gumleaf playing?'

'No,' I said. 'And I don't believe Foxy gave you the flu. You can't catch colds through closed windows.' I walked out of the front door to get away from his coughing. That's when I saw the note. A crumpled dirty envelope was lying on the porch. It said:

To the boy, with the long nose.

I tore it open. Inside was a message for me.

Sorry about the scratch, boy. I thought you was McFuddy.

McFuddy tore the note out of my hand. 'I knew it. I just knew it,' he spluttered. 'That low-down ratbag was up here last night and he gave me the rotten flu.' He ran inside and came out with the shotgun again. Once again he fired off both barrels down at Foxy's shack. The shot was answered straight away by another dull bang from Foxy in the valley below.

I tried to get McFuddy to explain what was going on but he was in a bad mood and wouldn't say anything about it. 'I'm straining a fence today,' he said. 'And I need your help. Grab one end of that corner post and we'll take it down to the bottom paddock.'

We staggered down the hillside with the heavy post. I was surprised at how strong McFuddy was. He didn't stop once but he coughed and spat the whole way. Then, just as we neared the fence line McFuddy stepped in a pat of fresh cow dung and slipped over. 'Ouch,' he screamed. 'My ankle. My ankle.' I rushed over to him and looked at his ankle. It was already starting to swell and turn blue.

'I'll help you back to the house,' I said. 'This looks serious.' I looked at his face. It was all screwed up with pain. Then, suddenly, a change swept over him and he grinned.

'Good,' he said. 'It hurts like the dickens. Just what I wanted.' He started to cackle like a chook that had just laid an egg. 'Go git me a stick boy. This is the best thing that's happened for a long while.' I found him a stick and he used it to help him hobble off to the road. He limped badly and I could see his ankle was hurting.

'Where are you going?' I asked him. 'You can't go off down the road with that ankle.'

'I'm going to the old twisted gum,' he called back

over his shoulder. 'And then I have some other business. You can go back to the house, boy, and don't you try to follow me.' He limped slowly down the road and finally disappeared round a bend in the road.

The whole thing was crazy. These two old men shooting at each other. And blaming each other for things they couldn't have done. And sneaking around playing tunes on a gumleaf in the middle of the night. I had to find out what was going on. So I followed McFuddy down the road, making sure I kept behind bushes where he couldn't see me.

4

I found it easy to keep up with him because he went so slowly on account of his twisted ankle. After about an hour he reached the old twisted gum he had pointed out to me the day before. I noticed all of the lower branches were stripped bare of leaves as if stock had been grazing on them. McFuddy hit at a branch with his stick and a leaf fell off. He put it up to his lips and blew. A strong musical note floated up the road. McFuddy laughed to himself and put the leaf in his pocket. Then he headed off down the road. I knew where he was going.

Sure enough, after about another hour of hobbling, McFuddy reached Foxy's shack. Foxy was peering into his telescope, which was pointed at our place. McFuddy crept on all fours along a row of bushes so he couldn't be seen. When he was quite close to the shack, but still out of sight, he grabbed the gumleaf and started to play a tune. I couldn't hear what it was because a strong wind was blowing but I found out later that it was 'Click Go The Shears'.

As soon as the first few notes sounded, Foxy jumped up in the air as if he had been bitten. Then he clapped his hands over his ears and ran inside screaming out at the top of his voice. McFuddy turned and ran for it. He bolted out to the road like a rabbit. I had never seen him move so fast. It took me a few seconds to realise he wasn't limping. His sprained ankle was cured. It wasn't swollen and it didn't hurt.

Foxy came out onto the porch carrying a shotgun, which he fired into the air over McFuddy's head. 'You're gone, McFuddy,' he shouted. 'I'll have you for goanna oil.' He tried to chase McFuddy up the road but he couldn't. He had a sprained ankle.

5

My head started to spin. This was the weirdest thing I had ever come across. These two old men seemed to be able to give each other their illnesses and cure themselves at the same time. By blowing a gumleaf where the other person could hear it. I decided to find out what was going on and I followed McFuddy up the dusty, winding road.

I caught up to him under the old twisted gum tree where he was sitting down for a rest. He was laughing to himself in his raspy voice. I could see he thought he had won a great victory. 'That's fixed him,' he said. 'That'll slow him down for a bit.' McFuddy didn't seem to care about me following him. In fact he seemed pleased to have someone to show off to.

'What's happened to your sprained ankle?' I demanded. 'And how come Foxy's got one now and he didn't have before?'

McFuddy looked at me for a bit and then he said, 'You might as well know the truth, boy. After all, you are family. It's this tree. This old twisted gum tree. When you play "Click Go The Shears" on one of its leaves, it passes your illness on to whoever hears it. But it only works for leaves on this tree. And the only tune that makes it work is "Click Go The Shears".'

It seemed too fantastic to believe but I had seen it work with my own eyes. 'Why does it only work with leaves from this old twisted gum tree?' I asked.

'I don't know,' he said. 'I've tried it with hundreds of other trees but it never works. It only works with this tree.' He gave an enormous sneeze and spat on the road. His nose was still red and his eyes were watering.

'Well, how come you've still got your cold?' I asked. 'Why didn't Foxy get that back just now when you passed on the sprained ankle?'

'You can't get it back again. The same thing can only be passed on once. After that you are stuck with it. I will just have to wait for the cold to go away on its own. And Foxy can't give me the sprained ankle back. He will have to wait for it to get better in the normal way. That's the way it works.' McFuddy took the gumleaf out of his pocket and threw it on the ground. I picked it up and tried to make a noise. Nothing came out. Not a peep.

'Save your breath, boy,' said McFuddy. 'Each leaf only plays once. After that it don't work any more.'

'Well, I think it's the meanest thing I've ever heard of,' I said. 'Fancy making another person sick on purpose. How long has this been going on?'

'Over sixty years, boy. And it's not my fault. Foxy first gave me the measles when we were at school. But I found out and I gave him a toothache back. That's how it all got started and it's been going on ever . . .' McFuddy stopped in mid-sentence. He was twisting up his nose and sniffing the hot, north wind. 'Smoke,' he yelled. 'I can smell smoke.'

He jumped up and started running up the road. 'Quick, boy,' he called out over his shoulder. 'There's a bushfire coming. Back to the house.' We both sped up the road as fast as we could go. We were only just in time. A savage fire swept over the top of the hill and raced through the dry grass towards the shack. Smoke swirled overhead and blocked out the sun.

'Git up on the roof, boy,' McFuddy yelled. 'Block up the downpipes and fill up the spouting with water. I'll close up the house.' I put a ladder up against the wall and filled up the spouting with buckets of water. McFuddy went around closing all the windows and doors. Then he started up a portable generator and started spraying the house with a hosepipe connected to his water tank. Soon the house was almost surrounded by fire. Sparks and smoke swirled everywhere. Spot fires broke out in the front yard and at the back of the house. Then the back door caught on fire. I beat at it with a hessian bag that I had soaked in water but it was getting away from me. McFuddy couldn't help. He was fighting a fire that had broken out under the front porch.

It looked hopeless. I couldn't hold the fire at the back door and I knew that at any moment the whole house would explode into a mass of flames. Then, without any warning, an old Holden utility sped through the front gate and stopped in a swirl of dust. It was Foxy. He jumped out of the car, put on a back-pack spray and rushed over to the back door. He soon had the flames out. Then he ran around to the front and started helping McFuddy on the porch.

The three of us fought the flames side by side for two hours until the worst of it had passed. Then we just stood there looking at the shack, which had been saved with Foxy's help, and the burnt grass and trees which surrounded us. The shack was saved but it was now an oasis in a desert of smouldering blackness.

6

McFuddy looked at his old enemy, who was still limping when he walked. He held out his hand. 'Thanks, mate,' he said. 'Thanks a lot.'

Foxy paused for a second, then he shook the out-stretched hand. 'It's okay, McFuddy,' he answered. 'I would have done the same for a wombat.'

McFuddy grinned. 'Come over and have a beer. You've earned it.' They both went into the kitchen and McFuddy opened two stubbies of beer and a can of Fanta for me. They were soon joking and laughing and talking about what a close shave it had been.

'I'm glad to see you're friends at last,' I said after a while. 'Now neither of you will have to visit the old twisted gum again.'

They both sprang to their feet as if someone had stuck a pin in them. 'The old twisted gum,' they shouted together. Both of them ran outside and jumped into the utility. I only just had time to climb into the back before it lurched off down the hill. I hung on for grim death and stared at the blackened, leafless trees that sped by us on either side. The car screeched to a halt and we all climbed out.

I was pleased to see the old twisted gum had been burnt in the fire. It was a black and twisted corpse. The leaves had all gone up in smoke. Except one. High up on the top, well out of reach, one lonely green leaf pointed at the sky. We all stood there looking at it and saying nothing. Then, without a word, Foxy ran over to the utility and drove off down the hill as fast as he could go. 'Quick,' shouted McFuddy. 'He's gone to git a ladder. Come and help me, boy. We must git that leaf before he does. It's the last one. Come and help me carry the ladder.'

'No way,' I said. 'I wish every leaf had been burnt. Passing on your sickness to someone else is a terrible thing to do. Carry your own ladder.'

'Traitor,' he yelled as he hurried off.

I sat there beside the blackened countryside looking up at the leaf. It was too high up for me to climb up and get it and anyway, the tree was still hot and smouldering. So I just sat there and waited.

I had been sitting there for quite some time when something happened. The leaf fell off its lonely perch and slowly fluttered to the ground. It landed right at my feet. I picked it up and put it in my pocket.

7

I was only just in time. At that very moment McFuddy and Foxy arrived carrying a ladder each. Foxy's car had conked out from overheating and both men were staggering under their heavy burdens. They dumped their ladders down and stared at the tree with their mouths open. Then they fell onto their hands and knees and started scrabbling around in the burnt debris at the bottom of the tree. 'The last leaf,' moaned Foxy. 'The very last leaf.'

'Gone, gone,' cried McFuddy. They scratched and searched everywhere but to no avail. They both became covered in black soot and dust. They looked like two black ghosts hunting around in a black forest.

After a while they slowed down in their search. McFuddy looked at me. 'The boy,' he said suddenly. 'The boy's got it. Give it here, boy.' They both started walking towards me slowly with outstretched hands. Their eyes were wild circles of white set in their black faces. They looked mean. Real mean. I felt like a rabbit trapped by two starving dingoes. I could see they would tear me to pieces to get their leaf. I pushed it deeper into my pocket and backed away.

I had to get rid of it. I wasn't going to give either of them the chance to get one last shot at the other. But I didn't know what to do. I was cornered. One of them was coming from each direction on the road and the paddocks were still hot and smouldering. Then I remembered what McFuddy had told me. Each leaf would only play one tune and then it wouldn't work any more. I decided to use up its power by playing it. I put it to my lips and blew. But nothing happened. Not a squeak. I tried again and a loud blurp came out. It was working. I tried to think of a tune to play but my mind was a blank. I was so nervous I couldn't think of one single tune. Except 'Click Go The Shears'. So that is what I played. It wasn't very good – there were a lot of blurps and wrong notes but it was 'Click Go The Shears', no worries.

McFuddy and Foxy fell to the ground screaming with their hands up over their ears. Then they put their hands over their noses. And so did I. My nose was normal. It had gone back to three centimetres long. And McFuddy and Foxy both had long, long noses. They had both copped my poor broken, stretched nose and mine was normal again.

McFuddy looked at Foxy's nose and started to

laugh. He rolled around in the dirt laughing until tears made little tracks through the soot on his face. Then Foxy saw McFuddy's nose and he started to laugh too. Soon all of us were rolling around in the dirt shaking with laughter.

8

McFuddy and Foxy didn't seem to mind their long noses and they made friends again once they realised there were no leaves left. I explained that both of them could have operations to shorten their noses but neither of them seemed very interested. 'I'm not trying to impress the girls at my age,' was all McFuddy said.

The next day I got on the train to go home. I wanted to get back to school again now I had a normal nose. It was a short holiday but it had turned out to be a good cure.

So there I was sitting in the train with the same people that I had arrived with. They were all staring at me out of the corners of their eyes trying to work out if I was that funny-looking kid they had travelled with before.

The ranger was the only one not taking any notice

of me. He was staring out of the window at the blackened forest. No one was listening to him except me. And I didn't like what he was saying.

'Never mind,' he rambled on. 'It will be green again this time next year. Gum trees usually spring back to life after a bushfire.'

Birdscrap

The twins sat on the beach throwing bits of their lunch to the seagulls.

'I don't like telling a lie to Grandma,' said Tracy. 'It wouldn't be fair. She has looked after us since Mum and Dad died. We would be in a children's home if it wasn't for her.'

Gemma sighed, 'We won't be hurting Grandma. We will be doing her a favour. If we find Dad's rubies we can sell them for a lot of money. Then we can fix up Seagull Shack and give Grandma a bit of cash as well.'

'Why don't you wait until we are eighteen? Dad's will says that we will own Seagull Shack then. We can even go and live there if you want to,' replied Tracy.

Gemma started to get cross. 'I've told you a million times. We won't be eighteen for another three years.

The last person who hiked in to Seagull Shack said that it was falling to pieces. If we wait that long the place will be blown off the cliff or wrecked by vandals. Then we'll never find the rubies. They are inside that shack. I'm sure Dad hid them inside before he died.'

Tracy threw another crust to the seagulls. 'Well, what are you going to tell Grandma, then?'

'We tell her that we are staying at Surfside One camping ground for the night. Then we set out for Seagull Shack by hiking along the cliffs. If we leave in the morning we can get there in the afternoon. We spend the night searching the house for the rubies. If we find them, Grandma will have a bit of money in the bank and we can send in some builders by boat to fix up Seagull Shack.'

'Listen,' said Tracy to her sister. 'What makes you think we are going to find the rubies? The place was searched and searched after Dad died and neither of them was found.'

'Yes, but it wasn't searched by us. We know every corner of that shack. And we knew Dad. We know how his mind worked. We can search in places no one else would think of. I think I know where they are anyway. I have an idea. I think Dad hid them in the stuffed seagull. I had a dream about it.'

'Hey, did you see that?' yelled Tracy without warning. 'Where did that crust go?'

'What crust?'

'I threw a crust to the seagulls and it vanished.'

'Rubbish,' said Gemma. 'One of the birds got it. Bread doesn't just vanish.'

Tracy threw another scrap of bread into the air. It started to fall to the ground and then stopped as if caught by an invisible hand. It rose high above their heads, turned and headed off into the distance. All the other gulls flapped after it, squawking and quarrelling as they went.

'Wow,' shrieked Gemma. 'How did you do that?'

'I didn't,' said Tracy slowly. 'Something flew off with it. Something we couldn't see. Something invisible. Perhaps a bird.'

Gemma started to laugh. 'A ghost gull maybe?'

'That's not as funny as you think,' said Tracy. 'It's a sign. Some thing or some one wants us to go to Seagull Shack.'

'Maybe you've got it wrong,' replied Gemma. 'Maybe something doesn't want us to go to Seagull Shack.'

The wind suddenly changed to the south west and both girls shivered.

2

Two days later Tracy and Gemma struggled along the deserted and desolate clifftops. They were weighed down with hiking packs and water bottles. Far below them the Southern Ocean swelled and sucked at the rocky cliff. Overhead the blue sky was broken only by a tiny white seagull which circled slowly in the salt air.

'How far to go?' moaned Gemma. 'My feet are killing me. We've been walking for hours.'

'It's not far now,' said Tracy. 'Just around the next headland. We should be able to see the old brown roof any moment ... Hey. What was that?' She felt her hair and pulled out some sticky white goo. Then she looked up at the seagull circling above. 'You rotten fink,' she yelled at it. 'Look at this. That seagull has hit me with bird droppings.'

Gemma lay down on the grassy slope and started to laugh. 'Imagine that,' she gasped. 'There are miles and miles of clifftop with no one around and that bird has to drop its dung right on your head.' Her laughter stopped abruptly as something splotted into her eye. 'Aaaaagh, it's hit me in the eye. The stupid bird is bombing us.'

They looked up and saw that there were now four or five birds circling above. One of them swooped down and released its load. Another white splodge hit Tracy's head. The other birds followed one after the other, each dropping its foul load onto one of the girls' hair. They put their hands on top of their heads and started to run. More and more birds gathered, circling, wheeling and diving above the fleeing figures. Bird droppings rained down like weighted snow.

The girls stumbled on. There was no shelter on the exposed, wind-swept cliffs – there was no escape from the guano blizzard which engulfed them.

Tracy stumbled and fell. Tears cut a trail through the white mess on her face. 'Come on,' cried Gemma. 'Keep going – we must find cover.' She dragged her sister to her feet and both girls groped their way through the white storm being released from above by the squealing, swirling gulls.

Finally, exhausted and blinded, the twins collapsed into each other's arms. They huddled together and tried to protect themselves from the pelting muck by holding their packs over their heads. Gemma began to cough. The white excrement filled her ears, eyes and nostrils. She had to fight for every breath.

And then, as quickly as it had begun, the attack ended. The whole flock sped out to sea and disappeared over the horizon.

The girls sat there panting and sobbing. Each was covered in a dripping white layer of bird dung. Finally Gemma gasped. 'I can't believe this. Look at us. Covered in bird droppings. Did that really happen? Where have they gone?' She looked anxiously out to sea.

'They've probably run out of ammo,' said Tracy. 'We had better get to the shack as quick as we can before they come back.'

3

An hour later the two girls struggled up to the shack. It sat high above the sea, perched dangerously on the edge of a cliff which fell straight to the surging ocean beneath. Its battered tin roof and peeling wooden walls stood defiantly against the might of the ocean winds.

Both girls felt tears springing to their eyes. 'It reminds me of Dad and all those fishing holidays we had here with him,' said Tracy. They stood there on the old porch for a moment, looking and remembering.

'This won't do,' said Gemma as she unlocked the door and pushed it open. 'Let's get cleaned up and start looking for those two rubies.'

Inside was much as they remembered it. There were only two rooms: a kitchen with an old table and three chairs and fishing rods and nets littered around; and a bedroom with three mattresses on the floor. The kitchen also contained a sink and an old sideboard with a huge, stuffed seagull standing on it. It had only one leg and a black patch on each wing. It stared out of one of the mist-covered windows at the sky and the waves beyond.

'It almost looks alive,' shivered Tracy. 'Why did Dad shoot it anyway? He didn't believe in killing birds.'

'It was wounded,' answered Gemma. 'So he put it out of its misery. Then he stuffed it and mounted it because it was so big. He said it was the biggest gull he had ever seen.'

'Well,' said Tracy. 'I'm glad you're the one who is going to look inside it for the rubies, because I'm not going to touch it. I don't like it.'

'First,' said Gemma, 'we clean off all this muck. Then we start searching for the rubies.' The two girls cleaned themselves with tank water from the tap in the sink. Then they sat down at the table and looked at the stuffed seagull. Gemma cut a small slit in its belly and carefully pulled out the stuffing. A silence fell over the hut and the clifftop. Not even the waves could be heard.

The air seemed to be filled with silent sobbing.

'The rubies aren't there,' said Gemma at last. She put the stuffing back in the dead bird and placed it on its stand. 'I'm glad that's over,' she went on. 'I didn't like the feel of it. It gave me bad vibes.'

As the lonely darkness settled on the shack, the girls continued their hunt for the rubies. They lit a candle and searched on into the night without success. At last, too tired to go on, Tracy unrolled her sleeping bag and prepared for bed. She walked over to the window to pull across the curtain but froze before reaching it. A piercing scream filled the shack. 'Look,' she shrieked. 'Look.'

Both girls stared in terror at the huge seagull sitting outside on the window sill. It gazed in at them, blinking every now and then with fiery red eyes. 'I can see into it,' whispered Gemma. 'I can see its gizzards. It's transparent.'

The lonely bird stared, pleaded with them silently

and then crouched on its single leg and flapped off into the moonlight.

Before either girl could speak, a soft pitter-patter began on the tin roof. Soon it grew louder until the shack was filled with a tremendous drumming. 'What a storm,' yelled Gemma.

'It's not a storm,' Tracy shouted back. 'It's the birds. The seagulls have returned. They are bombing the house.' She stared in horror at the ghostly flock that filled the darkness with ghastly white rain.

All through the night the drumming on the roof continued. Towards the dawn it grew softer but never for a moment did it stop. Finally the girls fell asleep, unable to keep their weary eyes open any longer.

4

At 10 a.m. Tracy awoke in the darkness and pressed on the light in her digital watch. 'Wake up,' she yelled. 'It's getting late.'

'It can't be,' replied Gemma. 'It's still dark.'

The shack was as silent as a tomb. Gemma lit a candle and went over to the window. 'Can't see a thing,' she said.

Tracy pulled open the front door and shrieked as a wave of bird droppings gushed into the room. It oozed into the kitchen in a foul stream. 'Quick,' she yelled. 'Help me shut the door or we'll be drowned in the stuff.'

Staggering, grunting and groaning, they managed to shut the door and stop the stinking flow. 'The whole house is buried,' said Gemma. 'And so are we. Buried alive in bird droppings.'

'And no one knows we are here,' added Tracy.

They sat and stared miserably at the flickering candle. All the windows were blacked out by the pile of dung that covered the house.

'There is no way out,' moaned Gemma.

'Unless . . .' murmured Tracy, 'they haven't covered the chimney.' She ran over to the fireplace and looked up. 'I can see the sky,' she exclaimed. 'We can get up the chimney.'

It took a lot of scrambling and shoving but at last the two girls sat perched on the top of the stone chimney. They stared in disbelief at the house, which was covered in a mountain of white bird droppings. The chimney was the only evidence that underneath the oozing pile was a building.

'Look,' said Gemma with outstretched hand. 'The

transparent gull.' It sat, alone on the bleak cliff, staring, staring at the shaking twins. 'It wants something,' she said quietly.

'And I know what it is,' said Tracy. 'Wait here.' She eased herself back down the chimney and much later emerged carrying the stuffed seagull.

'Look closely at that ghost gull,' panted Tracy. 'It's only got one leg. And it has black patches on its wings. And look how big it is. It's this bird.' She held up the stuffed seagull. 'It's the ghost of this stuffed seagull. It wants its body back. It doesn't like it being stuffed and left in a house. It wants it returned to nature.'

'Okay,' Gemma yelled at the staring gull. 'You can have it. We don't want it. But first we have to get down from here.' The two girls slid, swam, and skidded their way to the bottom of the sticky mess. Then, like smelly white spirits, the sisters walked to the edge of the cliff with the stuffed bird. The ghost seagull sat watching and waiting.

Tracy pulled the stuffed seagull from the stand and threw it over the cliff into the air that it had once loved and lived in. Its wings opened in the breeze and it circled slowly, like a glider, and after many turns crashed on a rock in the surging swell beneath.

The ghost gull lifted slowly into the air and followed it down until it came to rest on top of the still, stuffed corpse.

'Look,' whispered Tracy in horror. 'The ghost gull is pecking at the stuffed one. It's pecking its head.'

A wave washed across the rock and the stuffed seagull vanished into the foam. The ghost gull flapped into the breeze and then flew above the girls' heads. 'It's bombing us,' shouted Gemma as she put her hands over her head.

Two small shapes plopped onto the ground beside them.

'It's the eyes of the stuffed seagull,' said Tracy in a hoarse voice.

'No it's not,' replied Gemma. 'It's Dad's rubies.'

They sat there, stunned, saying nothing and staring at the red gems that lay at their feet.

Tracy looked up. 'Thank you, ghost gull,' she shouted.

But the bird had gone and her words fell into the empty sea below.

Snookle

Snookle was delivered one morning with the milk. There were four half-litre bottles; three of them contained milk and the other held Snookle.

He stared sadly at me from his glass prison. I could see he was alive even though he made no sign or movement. He reminded me of a dog on a chain that manages to make its owner feel guilty simply by looking unhappy. Snookle wanted to get out of that milk bottle but he didn't really expect it to happen. He didn't say anything, he just gazed silently into my eyes.

I placed the three full bottles in the fridge and put Snookle and his small home on the table. Then I sat down and looked at him carefully. All I could see was a large pair of gloomy eyes. He must have had a body but it was nowhere to be seen. The eyes simply floated in the air about fifteen centimetres above the bottom of the bottle.

Mum and Dad had already left for work so I wouldn't get any help from them. I gave the bottle a gentle shake and the eyes bounced around like a couple of small rubber balls. The gloomy expression was replaced by one of alarm and the eyes blinked a number of times before settling back to their original position.

'Sorry,' I said. 'I didn't mean to hurt you.' There was no reply, just a long reproachful look.

'Where did you come from?' I asked. 'And how did you get here? What sort of creature are you? What is your name?' I received no reply to my question. In fact, the eyes began to close. He was falling asleep.

A nasty thought entered my mind. What if he was dying? There is not much air in a milk bottle. He might be suffocating if he was an air-breathing creature. I thought about opening the bottle and letting him out. But if I did I could be in for big trouble. He might not go back into the bottle and he could be dangerous. He might bite me or give me some terrible disease that would kill off the whole human race. He might nick off, spreading death and disease wherever he went.

I went over to the window and looked outside. Maybe one of the kids from school would be passing. Two heads would be better than one, especially if the thing in the bottle attacked me. Then I remembered. It was Curriculum Day and there was no school. The only person in the street was poor old Mrs McKee, who was hobbling down her steps to get the milk. She wouldn't be any help. She had arthritis and it was all she could do to pick up one milk bottle at a time. It took her half an hour to shuffle back to the front door from the gate.

Some weekends I used to go and do jobs for Mrs McKee because her hands were so weak that she couldn't do anything by herself. Her garden was overgrown with weeds and her windows were dirty. All the paint was peeling off the house. I once heard Mum say that Mrs McKee would have to go into an old folks' home soon because her fingers wouldn't move properly. No, Mrs McKee wouldn't be any use if the eyes in the bottle turned nasty.

2

I looked at my visitor again. His eyelids were beginning to droop. At any moment he might be dead. I decided to take the risk. With one swift movement I took the metal cap off the bottle.

The expression in the eyes changed. They looked happy. Then they started to move slowly up to the neck of the bottle. I could tell that the little creature was climbing up the glass even though I couldn't see his body. The eyes emerged from the bottle and floated in the air just above the rim. He sat on the top of the bottle staring at me happily. I couldn't see his mouth or any part of his face but I knew he was smiling.

'What's your name?' I asked. It might seem silly to talk to an unknown creature as if it could answer but I had a feeling that he would understand me. Even so, I got a shock when he did answer. He didn't use words or speech. I could hear him inside my brain.

The word 'Snookle' just sort of drifted into my mind.

'Who are you, Snookle?' I said. 'And what do you want?'

Again he answered without talking. His reply melted into my thoughts. 'I am your servant. Your every thought is my command.' They weren't his exact words because he didn't use words but it is more or less what he meant. Especially the bit about my every thought being his command. That was the next thing I found out – he could read my thoughts. He knew what I wanted without me saying anything.

3

My stomach suddenly rumbled. I was hungry. The eyes floated across the table and over to the pantry. Snookle could fly. The next thing I knew a packet of cornflakes and a bowl flew slowly back with the eyes following close behind. Then the fridge opened and the milk arrived the same way. The cornflakes and milk were tipped into the bowl and sugar added. Just the right amount and just the way I liked it. This was great. He knew I wanted breakfast and he got it for me without even being told. I didn't eat it straight away because I like my cornflakes soggy.

I decided to try Snookle out on something else. I thought about bringing in the papers from the letter box. Snookle floated over to the front door and opened it. Then he stayed there hovering in the air. 'Go on,' I said. 'Out you go.' The eyes moved from side to side. He was shaking his head. I looked out the door and saw a man riding by on a bike. As soon as the cyclist had passed Snookle flew out and fetched the papers. I knew what had happened. Snookle didn't want anyone to see him except his master. I was his master because I had let him out of the bottle. He would only show himself to me.

I went back to my bedroom followed by Snookle. His preferred altitude was about two metres off the ground. I decided to wear my stretch jeans as there was no school that day. The moment the thought entered my mind Snookle set off for the wardrobe. My jeans, T-shirt and underwear were delivered by air mail and laid out neatly on the bed. The next bit, however, gave me a bit of a surprise. Snookle pulled off my pyjamas and started to dress me. I felt a bit silly. It was just like a little kid being dressed by his mother. I could feel long, thin, cold fingers touching me.

'Cut it out, Snookle,' I said. 'You don't have to dress me.' He didn't take any notice. That was when I found out that Snookle helped you whether you wanted it or not.

My nose was itchy. I could feel a sneeze coming on. As quick as a flash Snookle whipped my handkerchief out of my pocket and held it up to my nose. I sneezed into the handkerchief and said,

'Thanks, but that wasn't necessary.'

I went back to the kitchen for my breakfast. Snookle beat me to the spoon. I tried to grab it off him but he was too quick for me. He dipped the spoon into the cornflakes and pushed it into my mouth. I tried to stop him by keeping my lips closed but he prised them open with his chilly little invisible fingers and shoved the next spoonful in. He fed me the whole bowl of cornflakes just as if I was a baby.

Now I hope you will understand about the next bit. I am not really a nose picker but I have thought about it now and then. My nose was still a bit itchy and the thought just came into my mind to pick it. I wouldn't have done it any more than you would. Anyway, before I could blink, this cold, invisible finger went up my nose and picked it for me.

Snookle was picking my nose! I nearly freaked out. I screamed and tried to push him off but he was too strong.

After that things just got worse and worse. Snookle wouldn't let me do a thing for myself. Not a single thing.

4

I went back to the kitchen and sat down. This wasn't working out at all well. I could see my future looming in front of me with Snookle doing everything for me. Everything. He had to go. And quick.

I dropped a cornflake into the empty milk bottle and thought hard about getting it out. Snookle floated over and went into the bottle to get it. I moved like greased lightning and put the top back on that bottle before Snookle knew what had hit him. He was trapped. He didn't even try to get out but just looked at me with sad, mournful eyes as if he had expected nothing better.

Now I was in a fix. I didn't want to leave Snookle in the bottle for the rest of his life but I didn't want him hanging around picking my nose for me either. I looked out of the window. Poor old Mrs McKee had managed to get back to the house with one of her bottles of milk. Soon she would make the slow trip back to the letter box for the next one.

I picked up Snookle and slowly crossed the road. Then I put his bottle down outside Mrs McKee's house. I grabbed her full bottle of milk with one hand and waved goodbye to Snookle with the other.

His eyes stared silently and sadly back at me.

That was the last I ever saw of Snookle.

Over the next few days a remarkable change came over Mrs McKee's house. The grass was cut and the flower beds were weeded. The windows were cleaned and someone repainted the house. The people in the street thought it was strange because they never saw anyone doing the work.

I went over to see Mrs McKee about a week later. She seemed very happy. Very happy indeed.

About the Author

Paul Jennings is Australia's multi-award-winning master of madness. The Paul Jennings phenomenon began with the publication of *Unreal!* in 1985. Since then, his stories have been devoured all around the world. The top-rating TV series *Round the Twist* and *Driven Crazy* are based on his stories.

Paul Jennings has been voted 'favourite author' by children in Australia over forty times and has won every children's choice award in Australia. In 1995 he was made a Member of the Order of Australia for services to children's literature, and in 2001 was awarded the Dromkeen Medal for services to children's literature.